The McQuarries

Andrew Bagust

 A catalogue record for this
book is available from the
National Library of Australia

Copyright © 2021 Andrew Bagust
All rights reserved.
ISBN-13: 978-1-922343-62-8

Linellen Press
265 Boomerang Road
Oldbury, Western Australia
www.linellenpress.com.au

Dedication

Each one of us owes our existence to a long line of ancestors who laid down their lives to forge a great legacy for those who would follow. I would like to dedicate this book to Hector McQuarrie and the early pioneering families.

They sailed out into the Pacific with a dream and a prayer and, out of the raw materials from the ground, built our nations with their bare hands. Their courage, hard work, and resourcefulness allowed us the opportunity to boast how far we have come in 150 years.

Contents

Dedication iii

Contents v

Acknowledgments vii

Chapter 1 - The Midst of a Storm 1

Chapter 2 - May 93, Woman at the Helm 13

Chapter 3 - Ghost Ship 23

Chapter 4 - All at Sea 32

Chapter 5 - About the House 40

Chapter 6 - Back to School 46

Chapter 7 - Hector McQuarrie 55

Chapter 8 - Flying Cloud Debacle 60

Chapter 9 - Piracy and Gold 67

Chapter 10 - Tested with Fire 76

Chapter 11 - Scones with Uncle John 82

Chapter 12 - Lessons in the Office 90

Chapter 13 - Slavery & Black Birding 97

Chapter 14 - Strong Values 106

Chapter 15 - Shipping History 2 114

Chapter 16 - Meeting John and Harry 124

Chapter 17 - Storms on the Horizon 129

Chapter 18 - Message in a Bottle 139

Chapter 19 - Christian Women's Temperance 145

Chapter 20 - Women Win the Right to Vote 151

Chapter 21 - Wellington Versus Parnell 156

Chapter 22 - Bigotry and Judgments 162

Chapter 23 - Father's Bittersweet Return 168

Chapter 24 - Confessions and Mrs Vine 177

Chapter 25 - Catch Up Before They Leave Again 183

Chapter 26 - House For Sale 190

Chapter 27 - Election Day 196
Chapter 28 - Passions of Delight 207
Chapter 29 - Lions Face Off 217
Chapter 30 - All Together 225
Chapter 31 - Barbara's Passing 230
Chapter 32 - Death and Life 236
A Note From the Author 243
About the Author 248

Acknowledgments

Thank you for all those thousands of hours many of my family have spent collecting information about our wider family. It is certainly a labour of love that will last for generations to come.

- Gaye
- Junie
- Barbara
- Elaine
- Jack
- Rebecca

Thanks to Wendy and my lovely children for their help and encouragement.

Chapter 1

The Midst of a Storm

I grabbed the shroud ropes as I made my way along the ship to the little forward cabin, each step an effort as the boat pitched and rolled. The tiny steps down into the *Frank Guy's* cabin should have made me feel safe, especially as we were anchored in the harbour, but I knew that sound howling through the guy ropes for what it was. The storm was here. I lit the little stove, braced myself against the galley wall and fried some eggs while the cabin filled with smoke. Outside, Father methodically lashed down the ship. He must have checked the anchors three times in the last hour.

I shouted out of the cabin over the howling wind, "Father, take this! You need breakfast – it's warm against that cold blast. I'll bring hot tea!"

"Grand, lassie; it'll keep me going. This cold's cumin off the Arctic; I can smell it in the air. It gets into my arthritic hands and knees!"

Father was not so agile getting about the ship these days. He'd once said, laughing, "Me body will nay do what it used to!"

His heart still came alive at sea, but he struggled with the rope pulling, setting sails, and moving quickly about the ship. We had a fine crew, including Duncan, my old school friend, who climbed up Jacobs ladder like a monkey.

I stoked up the little cast iron stove again and invited the men to warm up, the rain now pouring down – Father came in looking like a drowned dog. I grabbed a linen cloth and dried him best I could.

"I am gunna have ye taken ashore. I'll have no argument and Duncan'll look aft ye. We've a long night ahead.

"Duncan, I am charging you to look after my bairn. You'll not let Phem' get wet … I don't want her coming down with fever."

"Yes, sir! Here, Miss, please take my coat. It's already warm. You heard what the Captain said!"

"Thank you, Duncan, you are so kind." I took the warm coat, which smelt of salt and sailor's sweat. "Come and get soup, you two."

Duncan stayed outside, so I passed his through the doorway. His warm hand touched my icy white hands. Father staggered around the galley, glad for shelter. He wrapped his hands around the hot tin mug.

"Ye gunna make me soft, lassie!"

"Father, at sixty-six, you are allowed a little fuss. Your face is blue with the cold."

"We had such a bonnie run, I thought our horizons were clear."

"What do you think it'll do, Father?"

"She blows where she will, lass. We've no choice. If we're lucky she'll blow herself out and we'll offload and be homeward bound. But those clouds last night looked like a demon had ploughed them in long furrows. She's ginna blow like a Banshee! It is imperative you stay dry in the cabin till we leave. I'll no' have ye getting cold … promise?"

"Yes, Captain!"

"Duncan will take ye ashore and find lodgings while we still can. High tide is 11am. Throwing for depth, we are in less than two fathoms. Perhaps this storm will hold back the tide. If it gets much worse, these anchors'll not hold in this sand."

We all had a sleepless night, with fore and aft anchors fighting one another, like strong men in a tug of war. The ship's timbers creaked with fury, cracking with eerie rhythm as the masts lurched back and forth. My wee swinging bed tossed back and forth, like watching lovers on a dance floor, the raging seas and crashing white waves tossing us wildly like a cork.

Father had rowed ashore at first light, even though the wind had destabilised the wee boat as it was lowered to the surface, and the swell had almost swamped it as it landed skewiff. Duncan had to bail ferociously to avoid successive waves sending her under.

The Captain found the Harbour Master, hoping a steamer might be due in the next few days. If we could unload in the next few days, we could get towed back out through the cut. Alas, the only steamer able to pull us out had left yesterday to aid another ship that had lost its rudder at sea.

"Father, did you have any success finding a work gang for offloading?"

"It's too late, lassie. Perhaps in a day or two. Winds coming from the east-south-east are forcing us ashore, I dunoo if the anchor'll hold till tomorrow … this harbour is far too exposed. This load of kauri could rip her apart if we go ashore."

"Father, we should have brought just the 96,000 feet to Ballarat and left the extra 40,000 feet for another day."

"What's done is done, lassie."

"I will pack my belongings now and, once ashore, send a

telegram home!"

"Phee, make sure you say nothing that will cause anxiety. I am praying we will save the ship."

Father had borne many losses in the last few years, there was only so much one man could take. "Father, we had such a great run, what are our chances of getting out?"

"The *Frank Guy* is a sturdy ship and has battled some terrifying seas running to and from Australia. But even she will not stand these monster waves hitting her broadside in this horseshoe bay. We might be lucky though, as it is a new moon in two days. If not, we will have little hope of getting her off before another high tide in four weeks!

"We were late getting in to tie her up at the new pier."

"This storm might smash us to pieces there anyway."

Father and I hugged. I kissed his prickly cold cheek. He never said a word but staring into those deep blue eyes spoke volumes as the wind now whistled through the ropes.

I grabbed my old trunk with its little gifts for the children and my personal belongings. McKay and Stubs, two burly mates swept me up like a feather and carefully helped me into the bow of the boat. Duncan sheltered me under a whaling coat and an old sail. They deftly lowered us into the breaking waters as old Frankie pitched and rolled in the foaming seas.

I took one last glance at Father's oil-skin hat lashed about his chin, the rain now pouring off his beard like a waterfall. He was in his element, pitting every ounce of his will against the storm.

Duncan strained on the oars, his muscles bulging as he deftly kept her course, trying desperately to tame the enraged sea which was like a whipped bull, driving us to shore. The little boat's light kauri construction makes her a strong, reliable craft, but I dared not look back at the huge breakers about to swamp us at any second. He created a rudder with one oar at the last minute, lest she broadside on the beach. Two men sheltering beside a tree ran out in their oil-skins and grabbed the boat to help us drag her up the steep shore. After grabbing my trunk, they flipped the boat over so she would not fill in the rain.

"Thank you, men!" I shouted over the wind. "Duncan, I'm headed up to ask about lodgings at the hotel." The sky was dark even though it was only early afternoon.

"I will go speak to some locals. You just stay warm!" he shouted back.

"You must go! Thank you, Duncan!" I stood shivering as rain ran down the back of my neck and, clutching my coat to my chest with my elbows, I looked out helplessly to that little ship on a raging sea. Then, dimly seeing the hotel looming through the mist, I hastened toward it.

The blustering wind carried me like a sail up the rise, each step difficult to keep my balance. It also did not help that I had that swaying sensation with my sea legs. The new hotel was a welcome sight, and by the number of windows, it boasted plenty of accommodation. As I opened the door, it flung wide on the wind and I fought to close it again. It was like stepping into a warm, hushed oasis as I made straight for the roaring fire.

Taking a deep breath, I warmed my frozen hands. They started to burn with chill blains immediately. I composed myself, straightened my hair and dress a little in the mirror over the mantelpiece, noticing in the reflection a mature, kind-looking woman gazing intently at me. She hurried from behind the counter with a dry towel.

"Good day ... you have a fine-looking hotel." I was trying

not to cough as I held a handkerchief over my mouth.

"Oh, thank you. You must be Miss McQuarrie? Are you okay, dear? What a frightful night – here take this and try and dry off a little by the fire."

She carefully lay the towel around my shoulders, and I hoped she did not suspect me of having consumption.

"The cold wind out makes me cough but it's warm in here with that fire." My face must have shown my surprise at her knowing my name.

"Your father's a regular up here, bringing the *Frank Guy* into harbour for a night, though we have not had a storm like this in many a long time. We held a room for you in case you came ashore. Will the Captain be joining you?"

"I'm not expecting him. He will batten down and wait it out."

"My son will make up the fire in your room. I have put you in the front room upstairs so you can keep an eye on the Captain. Why don't you come and get some hot soup when you are ready … you must be hungry."

"Oh, you are so kind. I was not aware till now just how hungry and exhausted I feel, but I must get to the telegraph office first?"

"You'll find it down at the post office. You might just make it before it closes."

"I know Father will be concerned for the children at home. Nothing seems to rattle him except his family's welfare."

I sat on the edge of the bed, gathering my strength before going to the telegraph office.

The message read. "*Great run. Arrived Woolgoolga NSW safely. Taking shelter to offload. All well. Home mid-September. Love, Phee.*"

In the calm of the dining room, the loud rattle and spatter on the windows was like some strange tribal music as the rain drove against the glass. There was a quiet murmur of other patrons who had come in like rabbits to a warm burrow. Mrs Pullen softly played the piano, a soothing balm to our strained nerves. The delicious smell of pea and ham soup wafted from the kitchen.

"Duncan! Over here!" I waved for him to join me. "Thank you for delivering my trunk up to my room. Come and sit down – you must be famished."

"I am, Miss, but I only notice it once I stop."

"Duncan, what's to become of us?"

He sat down at the little table. "Phee, the Captain's as tough as hobnail boots. This is what he lives for. He will come out of this; you will see."

He was right: The Captain was never more alive than in a storm. Duncan stared at me for a second and I thought about how long we had known each other. Our soup was delivered steaming hot to the table.

"Shall we give thanks, Phee? God is truly the master of storms."

As Duncan's warm hand took mine, I felt strangely secure. He gave thanks for our food and prayed for the safety of all on board. We had not sat together before and our conversation was easy. He finished his bowl of soup and, taking a hunk of bread, said, "I must be off now. Are you okay, Miss?"

"Yes, the fire and music will send me to sleep if I stay here any longer. I think I will go straight up to my room and get out of these damp clothes before I collapse into bed."

"Good for you. The Captain will need our support tomorrow. If you do not need me, I will get back to the ship; it will be a long night. I hope you can sleep.”

I still felt the swaying as I stood, and it seemed a long way up the grand staircase to my room. An orange glow from the fire flickered as I opened the door. The white sheets, already turned back, called me as I walked toward the heavy red rose-patterned drapes and the matching red floral bedspread. A washbowl and water jug set stood on the wooden sideboard, its marbled top white. A knock came on the door, and Master Pullen stood there with an arm-load of wood.

“Miss, here is a little more firewood; it will be cold tonight. Let me light your bedside lamp.”

“Thank you, Master Pullen. Please tell your mother this room is lovely.”

“Thank you, Miss. I will. Will that be all?”

“Yes, thank you. Good night.”

I could faintly see Duncan’s little boat cresting the top of a wave then disappearing into a trough. Father’s red lantern frantically swayed on the mizzen mast.

I tried putting out of my mind what would happen should an anchor fail as I poured water into the bowl and washed away the day with a flannel. Duncan was right, I needed sleep.

The curtains blew through the cracks in the window sash as I slid beneath the sheets and buried my head in a soft pillow to drown out the noise. *God watch over all our kin. Give Father strength and courage.*

I tried sleeping, but the rain clattered all night onto the glass, like hail. *Thwack! Thwack!* In the half-light, I woke, wondering where I was and heard a steady drip from the lapped ceiling boards. Almost in a stupor I rose and put the washbowl beneath the leak, feeling sick at the thought of father trying to save poor old *Frankie*. I stumbled to the heavy drapes, my heart pounding as I peered through the window. I tried desperately to make out the red swinging lantern, but all I could see was the silhouette of the three masts, which now seemed much closer to shore.

I placed another two logs of wood on the fire and told myself to sleep, somehow, as I crawled back into bed. It seemed like minutes later I woke. *Still dark. Is it morning? I cannot tell!* Throwing back the curtains, I braced myself for what I might find. The buffeting wind had not let up, and the lantern was gone.

I ran down the stairs; rushed out into the rain. The blast hit me, nearly blowing me over and I was instantly wet. I could not make out the dark shadow in silhouette. Was it another poor ship? I hardly noticed the gravel underfoot as I ran down the road to the beach. Her dark shape lay broadsided across the beach, stuck fast in the sand like a trapped whale. My gravest fears were confirmed as the waves continued to slam against her sturdy hull. But each enormous wave drove her further up the beach in the high tide. Duncan suddenly appeared and threw a blanket around me like Mother would.

He shouted, "This cold'll be the death of you! Go on back to your bed, there's naught can be done. We have worked all night, Phee. She threw the main bow anchors and at dusk broke the stern. We have lost the aft mast completely! She is stuck fast. We must pray she does not bust up with all that timber onboard. It is wracking the frame as she gets hammered on the beach."

Suddenly I noticed the sharp stony road and began to limp. Duncan's powerful arms picked me up like a stick and carried me back to the hotel. My nose was running from the icy blast. "Where's Father!?"

"He said he'll not leave the ship till daybreak. Go back to bed … your hands are like ice. We could be here for a few weeks, waiting for the next high tide and a powerful steamer to drag her off. When we can, we will unload the cargo to lighten her."

I tried to hurry up the stairs to my room, but my legs would not move; I tried wrapping the blanket around me, but my arms were frozen.

Suddenly I came to, and sat up stunned and shaking; completely disoriented. It was dark and the wind was blasting cold air into our room through an open window. My whole body was frozen. I floundered about hopelessly, looking for blankets that, through all my thrashing, had slipped over on Maggie's side of the bed. The dream seemed so real.

A wave of emotion flooded my heart and I burst out crying, sobbing from the depths of my soul. Like a child, I desperately wanted to run into Mother's arms.

"Phem, what is it? What is it?" Maggie said in a half stupor.

I could only make out the whites of her eyes in the moonlight, wide-eyed with fright. "It is not even real! It was a dream! Just a dream!"

Maggie, still a little confused, handed me a screwed-up hanky. "I have just had this terrible nightmare!"

She looked concerned as she hugged me gently, stroking my back. "Phee, what was it about?"

"I was Barbara? Duncan? What was *he* doing in my dream?"

"Phee, you are not making any sense! Don't wake Hannah."

I stared at her, trying to organise my thoughts. "Please, just close the window and I will tell you."

Maggie stumbled to the window, pulled the sash down

quietly so as not to wake the household.

"Last night … tonight," I reflected, "Father told me stories of ships that had been lost or wrecked. He told me in detail about the *Frank Guy* running aground in Woolgoolga last month with Captain Ferguson. I know Father wished he had been there instead, but of course, he was stuck in Melbourne saving the *Presto*! I thought I was Barbara on the ship with Father when it went aground!"

"I'm sorry, Phee. It is so unjust, after all he has suffered."

"I guess we are all feeling the cost of Father's plight. But Maggie, I feel he is not saying what is truly on his mind. Twice last night he looked like he was about to tell me something and did not. I feel it is not just the *Frank Guy* going ashore or the *Presto* wreck that is weighing on him. I suppose he is burdened about paying back his debts. Do you know it cost us a fortune – £700 in repairs to get the *Frank Guy* off the beach?"

Maggie nodded solemnly in the dark. "Imagine, we could buy a shoe store for that."

"Maggie! Father is also still waiting to find out about the insurance claim for the *Presto*, after that stupid captain of the *Bellinger* collided with him in Melbourne. We could lose everything!"

Hannah stirred in her sleep.

Maggie lowered her voice to a whisper again. "But Phee, won't they pay? I thought they exonerated Father of any fault."

"Yes. But it is still costly. If the skipper had not been distracted, they would not have gone straight to the bottom and the *Presto* would still be sailing now. Father told me last night they worked for two weeks to re-float her, but she was too badly damaged. Her stern and propeller were standing straight up out of the water. Actually, he also told me of another ship that just disappeared, never to be seen again!"

"It is freezing!" Maggie said, pulling up the covers. She gathered her hair and, tucking it over one shoulder, snuggled in behind me, "Like Father says, be still. The morning will be here soon enough."

As Maggie drifted off to sleep, the house was suddenly so quiet I could hear the familiar ticking of the grandfather clock. As I mulled over the events of the night, I wondered what tomorrow held. Father and Barbara would be gathering their last-minute stores before heading away. It occurred to me that these might be the last few moments of peace I would enjoy before taking on the burden of managing the house. I would need her support when Father left again – this burden would not be easy to bear. I took a deep breath and closed my eyes, allowing Maggie's words to soothe the dark clouds looming on the horizon.

Chapter 2

May 93, Woman at the Helm

Bess barked at the sound of the door handle. "Coo wee!" Mrs Davis's greeting suddenly filled the house with joyful spirit and warmth. *Bother! Is that the time already?* I glanced up to see the clock about to strike ten. Eileen brought her magic most days to transform our home and I usually fussed about in anticipation of her arrival. She swept in with her wand, splashing it about creating order out of chaos. This morning, sounds in the house reached their crescendo as the children spilled out the door to school, leaving a reign of sweet silence and a wake of chaos behind them.

Eileen's head popped around the corner of the kitchen door and caught sight of the blue sky through the double doors out to the harbour. Throwing her arms in the air, she exclaimed, "A perfect day! And good morning, Phee! Oh, look at you … the place is almost looking better than Barbara has it. Your Mother would be proud!"

"Ooh, I don't know about that. Barbara runs a tight ship." I scrubbed at a spot on the wooden table. *If only she knew.*

I recalled that Barbara was not terribly warm toward Eileen and her frivolous nature. There was jealousy there. Mother and Eileen had been close friends, having had Mary and Rosie the same year. Tragically though, tuberculosis also stole them only months apart.

"Now, where are they?"

"They needed a few things from Queen Street before they head off."

"Oh well, fair skies and a pinch of a light breeze from the west. A perfect recipe for the Captain's departure. If it stays like this for a few days, we will get our washing dry."

"Indeed." I stared blankly for a moment.

"The Captain is a master mariner, do not forget – if the wind and waves are favourable, he could be back by mid-August."

"I hope so, Eileen. If not, I pray he does not entertain the thought of another voyage before Christmas."

"Is not Christmas a sacred remembrance time for you all?"

I thought again of Mother, and at once my feelings began to betray me. I clasped my hands to hold it in. I turned away but tears rolled silently down my cheeks.

"Oh, deary, it sneaks up, doesn't it? Your mother was like a sister to me! It feels like *that* 29th of December was four months past, not four years. Christmas will always be a tough time for all of us."

She took a neatly folded handkerchief out of her apron pocket and, with a light stroke on my arm, gave it to me. Eileen felt a little awkward and took the kettle.

"Shall we make a pot of tea?"

"Yes, let me put the kettle on." I wiped my face and took the kettle from her.

"I will get on with a few little things first. Call me when its ready, Euphemia, and we will sit!"

"I would love that, especially today."

Eileen usually came with a cake, but today there was only a neatly-folded, wax-paper packet on the table. I unfolded one end and peeked in, slipping a shortbread out from under the wrapping. *I must be feeling a little emotional today* – like a bug blown in by a storm, limp and exhausted – I think it was my nightmare dream.

I closed my eyes and took a bite. *Mmm!* Buttery, crisp, sweet, melt-in-your-mouth shortbread. The tiny fork marks pressed into the top looked just like Mother's. I fought back the tears again as I stood savouring the moment. I spied my great-grandmother's precious bone china and decided that Eileen and I would celebrate Mother with a little tea party. I still had laundry suspended on the rack above the coal range.

I went and found Eileen sweeping leaves on the back path. "Eileen, leave that for the boys; that's their job," I said as we stepped back inside. "Would you like to sit here? It is the warmest seat next to the fire. I am sorry for all the laundry."

Eileen pulled a few things off the rack above her and started to fold some smaller items on her lap.

"Eileen, you are like a breath of fresh air, swooping in like a mother hen to rescue us."

The kettle started its low growl on the plate as I prepared the table, carefully sliding the cups out of the glass cabinet.

"I think you underestimate yourself, lass."

"The last time I fully managed Father's affairs, I was seventeen with Mary and Mother sick. Barbara had to step in to take over."

"You are twenty-two now and look how exceptionally well you have assumed this role alongside Barbara. Perhaps no one has expressed what a sterling job you have done, helping manage the house already from time to time. You show such energy and determination and take great care of the children. These winter rains make it taxing to dry heavy linen dresses for anyone."

"Oh, thank you, Eileen! But it does not come naturally to me."

I found Grandmother's beautifully embroidered Scottish linen cloth with the wee green leaves and purple thistles on each corner. Eileen softly touched the fabric.

"Where is this from?"

"Grandmother made it in Nova Scotia as a wee girl while being snowed in for months. It is the perfect size for this little table, isn't it?" The shortbread smelt wonderful as I laid pieces on a floral French tea plate that father had brought back from Caledonia.

"There is always work to do around the house with five of you to care for."

"Eileen, Mother and Barbara seem to toil with ease and content about the house. I am not sure I possess that same spirit."

"It is a thankless task managing a home, Phee. I really had no idea there was so much work to keep a house until I started work at twelve as a maid. I like helping someone else do their housework, more than doing my own."

We both laughed. "I could not imagine leaving home at twelve."

"Well, my parents were early missionaries here and we were poor when I was born. There was nothing here when they arrived in 1850. So I took work with a wealthy English family. But I still find, there never seems enough time to get everything done."

"Oh, yes! I have no longer packed the children off to school than the twins' dusty boots are coming back in the door. Perhaps it is not in my blood. My heart wishes to be on the high seas and my head in a book studying! Truly, is this all I can hope for? I feel invisible!"

Eileen moved about on her seat, not quite sure how to reply. "You have certainly inherited your father's passion for adventure, lass. I do love this china. I have looked at it in the cabinet many times and wondered where it is from?"

I wondered why Eileen changed the subject. *Perhaps she is reminded of her own passionate daughter.*

"The china is Mother's from Great-Grandfather McCleod. Apparently, just before Grandfather Kenneth sailed off forever bound for Nova Scotia, old Gran came out with two china cups and saucers off her table. They were wrapped in this cloth and placed in a little wooden box Great-Grandad had made. It is carved with the hills of Scotland and a scene of purple heather blowing in the breeze on the lid."

"What a treasure ... they are beautiful!"

"The thing is, Eileen, I remember when I was completing my proficiency, I held much higher aspirations for my life. I have dreamed of running my own business which is the only way a woman can provide her own means. Men seem to have all the say. If Father were lost at sea, what then?"

"Oh, God forbid! You have been asked to assume an extremely difficult role, but it will only be a few years and the children will be grown up and you will be married!"

"Do I have to marry? Will I ever marry? I am stuck here!"

Eileen flushed. "You are so fortunate. This is a beautiful home. And the Captain is a great provider."

"This house makes me sad sometimes. There are many happy memories but also grief. I want to escape like Barbara off to sea. It is like black clouds of sadness sneak up on me, quite unexpectedly ... like some black bear pounces on my chest with gripping pangs of deep sadness."

"You have suffered so many losses over the past few years. I have those feelings when I remember my Rosie. I try to recall the sound of her voice but that too is almost gone. Tears will roll down my cheeks when I am doing the most trivial things as my mind is free to wander, then I try to keep busy to take my mind off it."

"Eileen, I am never going to replace Mother the way Barbara has." I mindlessly re-arranged a vase of flowers and threw out the dead ones.

"Phee, I know you love to fuss over the children. I suspect it could be more about missing your mother than being a mother?"

"It is like these dead flowers – one minute you are glorious and the next …!"

"I know you miss her dearly! I sometimes find something will just set me off. Like the smell of scorched linen when I am using the hot iron, mindlessly doing your girls dresses."

"I am sorry, Eileen; I would never have thought of that reminding you of Rosie."

"It seems like only days ago those pudgy little fingers were helping me mix shortbread. Ohh! the alluring smell of freshly baked shortbread biscuits cooling on the table?" Eileen closed her eyes, imagining it as she gently smelt her piece before taking a bite.

"Mine is just seeing a hairbrush sitting on my dresser. Mother's nimble fingers would carefully clear it after softly running it over my thick hair, stroking my head with each move. Sometimes I sneak into my mother's room, and when nobody is around, I bury my face in her favourite shawl. It makes me feel like a little girl again laying on her chest, listening to the soft swish of her heart. The other night I dreamt I had climbed into mother's warm bed and was wrapped in her arms. It was so real; I was startled when I woke to the sound of the boys chasing about the house and the sun streaming through my window. I desperately wanted to be transported back into my dream again."

"Oh, my dear, I have had similar dreams of Rosie. You and your mother were close. You can never replace her, but you can remind the children about how wonderful she was."

"She gave everything. I am not sure that I can." I slowly sipped my tea while Eileen waited for me to continue.

"Eileen, I hold a terrible secret to my heart. I have not spoken of it all these years. It causes me terrible anguish and struggle!"

"What is it, dear?"

"I feel such anger toward Mother for leaving us!" I could feel my cheeks flush and a dam about to burst inside. "How can my heart harbour such darkness when I loved her so much!" My whole body trembled and shook with deep sobs as I buried my face in Eileen's bosom. "I feel guilty! If only I had nursed Mother and Mary instead of Barbara, she would still be teaching instead of fighting tuberculosis?!"

"My dear, you were only seventeen!" Eileen took my face and kissed it. My whole body was awash with love as she enveloped me in her arms. I wanted to linger there forever. I surrendered my gaze to her deep brown eyes.

"This darkness and deep loss you feel, and wanting to spare Barbara, only proves your love. I too held guilt for years that, somehow, I could have done more for Rosie. I think Annie is smiling on you right now."

She bowed her head for a second "God, how could you have taken Annie when we all needed her so much. Lord, help us understand your ways, amen.”

I suddenly felt like a crushing weight had been lifted. I took a deep breath and tried to gather myself. As we rose to our feet, Eileen took my hand.

“You cannot be your Mother or Barbara, you can only be yourself.”

I stared at her in relief – she was right. “All of this because of a few biscuits!” We laughed together, then Eileen glanced at the clock.

“Sorry, dear, I must go. I have that roast at home to prepare! Will you be alright? I will come by tomorrow.”

“Yes, I will be fine!” I hugged her and thanked her and followed her to the door. Bess jumped up to see what was happening.

Eileen squeezed my hand and said, “Thank you for the tea party. Come over any time.” She kissed me on the forehead and strolled to the side gate. I had so wanted to tell Eileen about my dream and about Duncan.

Feeling suddenly strengthened, I stacked all the folded clothes, as if cleaning and sorting these troubles was like laying them finally to rest. I said out loud to myself, “Euphemia McQuarrie, it is time to take charge!”

I threw off my apron and rushed to change before Ruby arrived. We had decided at music practice to meet for tea and cake. She was such fun, talking ninety-to-the-dozen and was quite mischievous wearing bold dresses with puffy sleeves, matching sashes and bright ribbons on her hat. I knew how much she spent – she was quite spoilt. Anyway, it was a healthy distraction to have a little space before Father headed away on the high tide the following week. I felt a little more relaxed as well because Magg and Barb were cooking dinner that night.

I found a warm spot on the porch and picked up yesterday's *Auckland Star* Father had left, read it while I waited for her. The news was all about the elections. Ruby and I had been secretly going to a few Temperance meetings with Aunt Christine and Aunt Sarah.

An article read:

> *We are most desirous that The Earle of Glasgow will sign the new bill of law allowing women to vote.*

I could not believe it! Could it really happen!?

The gate squeaked, and Ruby came round the corner in pink, through the rose-covered arch, blending in perfectly with a spray of bright pink roses. She threw her arms around me as if she'd not seen me in weeks.

"Oh, Phee, are they really going away again? How long is it this time? Do you think Barbara will bring back any of the latest fashions from Melbourne? It is not all bad them going away, perhaps we could invite John and Master Kelly over for tea?"

"Ruby, slow down. They have not even left yet. Besides, inviting them with my brothers and sisters at the table, I think not! You are quite wicked, you know."

"Oh, you think I am wicked! Remember the last time the Captain and the Teacher sailed?"

"Ruby, I am not about to compromise my social standing over an afternoon tea party. You know I need to steel my nerves and get busy when Father sets sail, staying up late when the house is quiet."

"You love to read."

"Well, yes, but for me, it is fatal to pick up a book and read for even a minute. I am transported to another world and before I know it, my candle is spluttering and it's four in the morning."

"Phee, you *look* like you stayed up all night. You are quite white."

"Ruby, I slept terribly." I relived the awful nightmare of the *Frank Guy* going aground in Woolgoolga, only I was Barbara and Father was the Captain.

"But was it not another captain who sent her aground? What were *you* doing in it as Barbara?

"It doesn't matter. He stayed up late telling me stories, last night. The weird thing is Duncan McKenzie was in my dream!"

"Little fat Duncan from school? What was he doing there? I did not know you even liked him! Do you?"

"No! I have never thought of him that way until now. The way he whisked me into his arms, saving my feet from the stones on the road, made my heart pound. Mind you, it was a dream."

"Phee, you have never spoken of him once. Does he not work for your father at the yard?"

"I see him from time to time and he is always polite. He is definitely not fat now!"

We sat talking well into the afternoon. I could not help feeling jealous that she was free to do whatever she wished. Her father had made his fortune selling real-estate to all the settlers coming from Great Britain. He provided Ruby a lifestyle that allowed her freedom to be frivolous.

Chapter 3

Ghost Ship

I quickly tried to finish the repairs to Maggie's dress in the last of the warm sunlight streaming through the sitting room window. The hem had torn as it snagged on a boot cleaner outside the corner store. She returned quite ruffled as she had just gone to pick up a few things for dinner.

As I glanced up, Father appeared as a shadow in the doorway, looking like he would say something but did not like to ask. He was wearing his favourite brown checked waistcoat and suit jacket. It looked a little tired and worn out, like him.

"I think it's high time you got another jacket, Father. Didn't Mother have that one made for our portrait pictures?"

"Yes, but you'll not be fitting me with any new suits. This one is finally comfortable even if it has shrunk slightly. Times are tough, lass. I have even had to let some good men go in the last few days. It seems to me you girls hand on a dress just as it is becoming comfortable." Father smiled.

"I don't think it has shrunk. You are just spoilt by all the lovely meals your daughter's make! If we can spare it, please let Barbara do a little shopping for us before you return." I said, smiling back.

"I will see."

He turned to leave then looked again. "I love this old waistcoat. It reminds me of the day Annie took me off for a fitting. She said, '*They cut it to the latest European styles and colours!*'"

"Styles from twenty years ago!" It was great to see Father laughing about something Mother had said. "Well, those woollen trousers are the worse for wear. Perhaps you could go with Barbara and buy something in Melbourne?" Father's face again looked worried. "What is it, Father"?

"Melbourne. About that. We have had to change our schedule and leave earlier than expected with this shipment to Victoria."

"When will you be leaving?" I asked pensively.

"Probably tomorrow. We need to head away as soon as the ship's cargo hold is full. The men have been loading for a few days already. The weather is likely to be settled for the next week, but, unfortunately, I had also promised to speak in Maggie's history class about the impact of the shipping industry in Auckland."

"Barbara is the teacher. Could she not do it when you return?"

"I had thought that she might enjoy going back into a classroom for a few days. But I had not expected her to be travelling with me! You see, they are studying it right now and it is all arranged. Would you do it?"

"*Me!*" I was horrified "Not in Mrs Laird's class!"

"Yes. Would *you* consider going and speaking to her class on my behalf?"

"Father! Let me just say she and I do not share similar views about some things. Anyway, I do not know enough of our history to be of any real help! I am certainly not used to standing up in front of a whole classroom to speak. How would Maggie feel if I made a fool of myself?" Any excuse would do because I did not like Mrs Laird and I had not spoken to a room full of fifteen-year old's before.

"You spoke well a few weeks ago when you were asked to give the reading in church. I have also heard you tell many stories to the children in the past. You have a gift; you might surprise yourself. Just do not start talking about the Temperance movement or woman having the right to vote."

Father's eyes were smiling as he looked at me, his grin cheeky. I took the bait anyway. "You will see, Father, it is going to be a whole new world for women. I am going to speak up for our cause any way I can! Things must become more equal."

"So, you will do it then. I could almost see you going into politics for a cause," he said, laughing.

My mouth opened but momentarily no words came to me. "I walked right into that, did I not?" I finally replied. I should have learned by now not to bite. "Anyway, I did feel nervous in church, but I made sure just to focus my attention on Ruby."

Lassie, in many ways you would be a better speaker than I would. You are closer in age for one thing. I think Maggie would feel proud. You already know much of our history and I could help you prepare tonight after supper."

I could see the troubled look on Father's face and decided to keep to myself what a terrible nightmare I'd endured during the night after listening to his story of the *Frank Guy*. Although I did not let on, I had secretly been doing a little public speaking when attending our Franchise League events. I put down the needle and went to Father, wrapped my arms around him. "I love your tales of the high seas! Is that all that is troubling you?"

"That's my girl! You are a bonnie lass!"

He gave me a hug and sighed heavily as he held me. "Father, are you okay? I feel like this is not the only thing that is worrying you."

I caught his glance, but only for a second, like a small boy who'd been found out for stealing a biscuit. He stared directly at me and, taking a big breath, went to speak but just then Hannah, who had not let Father out of her sight all day and now leaned against the door jamb, said as she approached:

"Father, will you come and speak to my class too?"

He scooped Hannah up in one graceful sweep, knocking over the candelabra on the sideboard. "You, little scallywag Maisy. I think it'll be a few years till you do history lessons in secondary school ... but how about we tell a few stories over supper tonight? Come and help your sisters set the table."

He tossed her on his shoulders, and they went off to the dining room. Father sometimes called her Maisy, the way Mother did, but I'd never asked why.

Barbara and Maggie had made a special dinner of roast lamb. Hannah quietly set the table, twirling from one place setting to the next like a ballerina. *I really must take her back to ballet lessons with Mrs Bechovic, she is delicate on her feet.*

Our private dining room was next to the front sitting room and had a spectacular view of the harbour. I never tired of the changing scenery looking far out to the islands in the gulf through the double doors. They had heavy linen drapes with bold pink flowers hanging from deep pelmets of the same floral fabric.

I replaced the candles in the candelabra, cleaned up the wax, straightened up the silver cutlery, which was on Mother's favourite Scottish linen, ready for supper. I stood for a moment, listening to the sounds of laughter throughout the house, and thought how happy Mother would be if she could catch a glimpse of us tonight all sitting around the table together.

The three boys were now coming through the scullery jostling and elbowing their way through. The twins were often in their own little world and, if they were quiet, then you had to worry.

Barbara said, "Boys, be careful. Don't drop one of those plates, you'll have Maggie to deal with."

We all laughed. It was a fine roast meal of lamb, pumpkin, potatoes, peas, and a jug of gravy, on Mother's china plates. It was quite a spread this night, our meals having become humble over the last few months.

Dugald and Ken always fought for the window seat so they could recognise the ships' lanterns and flags coming into the harbour, especially if the conversation was disinteresting. They could recognise a particular ship by its mast and would quietly mutter the ship's name, kicking each other under the table if they disagreed.

"Murdoch, please take your elbows off the table, and Ken, stop kicking your brother."

Father always sat at the head and would bow his slightly balding head to give thanks for our meal, while the boys did their best not to stab each other under the table with a fork or some such thing. We all held hands when Father prayed.

"Let us give thanks," Father said as he began to pray. "Lord, thank you for this beautiful feast that Barbara and young Maggie have prepared. Thank you for your many blessings, give us health and keep us all safe." He finished as we all chorused, "Amen!"

"Father, please tell us one of your stories!" said Dug.

Father, who had been shaking salt on his meal, stopped for a second and looked at Dug. "Let us be having you then." He smiled, looking at each of us as he held up his fork of lamb dripping with gravy. "You are a fine crew; mother would be so proud of this wee ship. We will clear up first."

In no time at all we were finished, and after clearing away the plates, we sat around on the lounge floor rug. The children's faces looked eager as Father proceeded with his story. The trouble had gone from his face, and instead, the sparkle had returned to his eyes, catching the magic in the candlelight as he did the thing he loved most.

"One night we were sailing back from Caledonia in the schooner *Fiery Cross*, via Norfolk Island, when we became calmed. There we were in the middle of the ocean. All the sails lay limp on her three masts. It was one of those dark eery moonless nights.

"Mac was throwing out the depth gauge from time to time and phosphorescence danced like pearl necklaces running down the line into the dark deep. All of a sudden, a heavy *thud* shook the whole ship and some of the men were thrown to the deck. From the starboard bow, there was a *Thud! Thud! Thud!'* Father had stomped his foot on the floor three times, giving us all a fright! Murdoch roared with laughter.

"We grabbed a lamp off the Boson's deck and ran to investigate, thinking we had hit rocks. As the light swung around, across the sea a huge dark monster loomed in front of us, against the bulkhead."

We gasped, sitting with eyes wide open, motionless like statues waiting for Father to continue as he took a slow breath.

"There are true stories, children, of huge snake-like creatures witnessed in the deep. Many years ago, a ship's crew swore on what they had seen in the Indian ocean, water so deep it cannot be measured. A *huge* snake, three and a half feet thick with scales and spines along its back, had a whale in a vice-like grip. The sea was like foam as they thrashed and wrestled, going down then bursting up again. They spun over and over in the waves, as the whale smashed its tail on the water. Each slap was like a cannon blast. The snake would not let go and slowly the whale tired, and the tail stopped thrashing. The snake had beaten its prey. The whale had lost, and they disappeared again down into the deep."

The children had been holding their breath, and suddenly let it out.

"Instead of a sea monster, an enormous hull – a ghost ship – lay right on the bow. We stared for a few minutes watching the phosphorescence dance around the edge of the hull as water lapped against her timbers. We were not quite sure we believed our eyes. It was like it had risen from the depths of the sea. The upturned hull was covered in barnacles and seaweed which was growing from its edges. Sea worms were slowly eating her timbers away."

Dugald's face reflected his imagination was going wild. "Father, it was like a floating island … what did you do?"

As soon as we regained our composure, we made a plan to sink her. We could not just leave it floating around in the ocean currents. Another unlucky sailor could collide with her, fully set and go straight to the bottom. We slung a rope on one of the shipwrights and sent him out with an axe. In no time at all he had cut a sizeable hole in the ship. We were expecting a whale spout of water to gush out as he broke through, but nothing happened. We hauled Mac on aboard again and watched as she floated past. You see, she was full of timber and could not be sunk.

"So, what did you do, Father?" Murdoch asked.

"The best we could do was set her free again and hope she

was wrecked on some coastline. We watched silently as she slowly bumped along the ship's starboard, catching the light of our swaying lamps till she disappeared into the darkness."

"What was the name of the ship, and how long had it been like that?"

"Ken, her name was the *Kentish Lass,* and she had disappeared two years ago. She was fully loaded with timber but never arrived in NSW. It was a sobering thought. If God had not let us be calmed, we might have hit her in the darkness and gone straight to Davey Jones locker."

"What is Davey Jones locker?" Dug asked.

Father chuckled nervously. "Some sailors say you go there when you die."

Quick as a flash, Maggie said, "I'm not going there! I want to be with Mary and Mother."

"Father, do you think there are ghosts still aboard?"

"I don't know, Dug, but I dare say, there could be bones of sailors trapped in the hull. Aharrhh!" Father grabbed Hannah's ribs on his lap and she squealed.

"We are not scared!" said Ken

Father told one story after another until all the children were finally in bed.

We talked well into the night about adventures and sad tales of lost sailors and wrecked ships. It was a rare moment to spend time with Father, he had been away for so much of our lives. He went over the current shipping manifests and accounting records at his desk should any customer need to settle or inquire about cargo to be shipped.

"You can send me a telegram if you need – you have my address in port."

"Father, you will tell me if there's something I need to

know?"

"Phee, you have enough to think about already, managing the house and it's already late. I will speak to you about it when I return."

"I know something is troubling you. I have seen you nearly tell me a few times. What is going on?"

"It is probably nothing, but it can wait till I return."

I held his gaze for a second before hugging him tightly.

"I love you, Father! I must get to bed." I turned and quietly made my way along the hallway on the creaking floors, wondering now what could worry Father that much.

I tried not to wake Maggie as I slipped into the warm blankets beside her. I was feeling many emotions at the thought of managing the house again. It was like I had climbed out of a chrysalis, about to spread my wings for the first time. I needed to take charge of something. My head was awash with Father's stories and sacrifices that Mother and he had shared. I wondered what had driven this man to use all his talents and passion to provide for us and his many men.

Perhaps for the first time, I could see that Father had also suffered being away at sea. His heart torn by grief losing so many he loved. But I could not shake off the thought that he had something he could not share.

Chapter 4

All at Sea

It was icy cold in the morning with frost on the front garden. The Captain had been up before dawn gathering his last few things and had the fire going. He looked troubled as he went about the house. Even his old boots sounded tired on the wooden floors. He threw a few logs on the fire and rubbed his balding head as if the creases in his forehead might disappear. He always did this when he worried. I had seen that look all too many times in the last few years.

"Father, come and have tea; I have made a pot."

"Thanks, lass, I will take it as I work as I still have many things to organise."

Father called out to Barbara, who was staring silently into her immaculately arranged trunk. "Have you seen my spectacle? I had it in the study going over those charts again last night."

"No, Father. Is it in the sitting room?" she replied.

Maggie came out yawning and sat with me, mirroring the anticipation welling up in my heart. We watched Barbara pack her last few things.

Maggie whispered, "She'll be a great support to Father. She has his stubborn strength, and few things seem to rattle her. She has run a tight ship managing this house like a headmistress. Imagine poor Father!" We laughed nervously.

"I will still miss her when she's away. She makes it look easy."

"I was only eleven when mother passed and never noticed there was so much to do."

"Maggie, even at nearly eighteen, I watched Barbara almost seamlessly assume the role of running the house as she took over nursing Mother and Mary till they passed."

"She's suffered through all the bankruptcy trials in '88 as well! It will be different: you are not like her at all. You are more impulsive, emotional and verbal."

"We can team up together. The twins especially always seem to make excuses to get out of household chores."

"You are right. The boys are not expected to do much, but they are always out playing games. At least we can depend on Murdoch to be sensible. I sometimes end up chopping wood myself. It does take out my frustrations and speeds up getting dinner prepared. I flatly refuse to empty our night cans or bring in the milk cans anymore!"

"Shall we make a pact, Phee, that we will do our best to steer them toward doing an equal share?" We slapped hands together, laughing.

"Sounds good!" And it did feel good to have Maggie's companionship. She was quite mature sometimes.

Barbara came through. "Phee, remember to dose the children with cod-liver oil or spoons full of malt. Make sure they wear scarves and warm hats."

We were all terrified deep down about getting consumption. Trying not to talk about Barbara being sick, we had all heard her smothered coughs in the night through the walls.

"Of course, Barbara, and I will give them small amounts of rat poison when they are naughty."

Barbara swung around in horror; looked at me wide-eyed.

"Barbara, it will be fine. They will be sick of me within a few weeks."

She called out as she walked briskly toward her room, "That is not funny or something to joke about."

"At least Barbara will get plenty of fresh air. I could not bear the thought of her …"

"Maggie!"

"What?"

"I know what you were going to say. Promise me you'll not talk like that, especially in front of the younger children."

"We all know …"

"Yes, but it is not something we even want to contemplate right now!"

"Bess, stop barking and get down from the door. She always barks when Nikolai comes."

"She wags her whole body with excitement and leaps onto his cart, hoping he has a small bone for her."

"He usually does! That is why she is overweight."

Father bent down and fondly scratched Bess behind the ears. He said, "Now you take good care of my bairns, Bessie!" She stared into his eyes as if understanding every word. He turned and picked up Hannah, holding her to his hip.

She played with his wild beard. "Father, your whiskers are prickly!"

He looked resigned as he checked his pocket watch. Putting Hannah down, he took his old brown leather bag and ship's log folder. These were the most familiar things I had seen in his hand over the years. The Captain said a prayer over us as he left and gave us all a kiss on the cheek.

"Lord, give Phee strength and wisdom to care for our

family, watch over each one till we are home again, Amen!"

My smile belied the feeling of insecurity in my heart.

Father gripped Murdoch by his forearms, "Son, look after your sisters. You are the man of the house while I am gone." He roughed up the twin's hair. "Behave, boys!"

Barbara kissed my forehead and called me by my full name. "Euphemia McQuarrie, remember if you need anything you can ask Mrs Davis or Aunt Christine?"

"Thanks, Barbara, you don't have to worry. The three boys still have two mothers with Maggie and …" I took Hannah's hand, "… three if you count Hannah," I said to tease her a little.

Barbara smiled, her eyes saying all the things she was holding back.

"Just keep your chest warm, and if the Captain gets gruff, just put extra sugar in his tea," I said in jest.

"And if he is naughty? Rat poison?' Barbara tried to laugh but covered her mouth coughing. She climbed up into the carriage, clutching her soft bag to her lap.

"I will send word as soon as we reach Melbourne."

We waved until the cart disappeared over the crest of Salisbury Road hill. I fought back tears as I watched Maggie's eyes well up.

"Emmie, how long will Father be away?" Hannah said.

The children all turned to hear the answer. "I do not know, Maisy, about forty sleeps – shall we start counting them off? … We could start a little diary today to tell Father all the things we have done while he is away. It is a good chance to practice your writing."

"What date is it today?"

"It is Friday, the 26th of May 1893."

"How do you know that?"

"Nicolai got me to say it over and over to remember it."

"You are very clever!" I watched Maggie go quietly off to our room. "Come on, Maisy. Let us make a pot of tea!

"Where does he go?"

"Father's been sailing to the Clarence River and back full time in the last few months. Barbara has only been away twice on shorter trips to Greymouth. This time the first load is going to Ballarat in Victoria."

We had all been mulling about on the porch hoping to spot the sails heading out.

I was busy making hot cocoa with the children, stirring it on the stove when we saw a flash. "Quick, children," I shouted, as her white wings came into view. Suddenly a herd of feet came from every corner of the house. We all watched from the porch as the *Frank Guy's* three masts filled with sails now starting to billow sailed away out to the open sea.

"Phee, look how low she is in the water!"

"She's carrying kauri for our shipyard in Thames, then she'll fill up from there again and head to Melbourne, where Father will return with coal from the Clarence."

We watched her slowly sail out past the islands until her white wings had flown away.

"Why did Barbara have to go?" said Ken

My mind raced to think of a reason why Barbara had gone. "Ken I know you always miss her – we all do – but she's had to help Father as he is finding it hard to get around the boat now. Besides, the fresh air will be good for her."

"Emmie, do you think Barbara will bring us something back?"

"We will have to wait and see. Have you ever known her to

come home empty-handed? Remember last time … she had gifts for the boys, a bright pink hatbox for Maggie, some white crinoline fabric for you and when she opened her old sea chest, she had a paper parcel for me." I began to twirl as if wearing my beautiful dress. "Inside the crisp white tissue was a glorious blue taffeta dress. I didn't want to take it off, and oh how Master Earle blushed when I bid him good morning the first time I wore it to church."

"Will I get to go to Melbourne one day?"

I lifted Hannah to my knee as we sat waiting for the kettle to boil. "Maisy, it is a big bustling city, with fine buildings, beautiful parks and shops full of dresses and shoes. I still remember a few years back when Father took my hand, and we walked the streets of Ballarat together. That town of gold. It was just after Mother passed away. I was so excited boarding my first train. It had seemed like floating on air as the wheels went clickety-clack. And we sped along faster than a rabbit being chased by a dog." I jumped up and chased the children around the room. "You will get to go one day!"

"What happened then?"

"We visited some of Father's timber merchants who were extremely busy with buildings going up everywhere.

"Maggie's class is studying shipping, and do you know, Father said there's one company in New South Wales making ship's masts out of our tall kauri logs, and they cannot keep up with demand. Father says we need to be thankful for all the houses, ships and furniture being built in the colonies because it gives us income!

"As we walked along the main street, I kept stopping to look in the candy shop or bakery. Father gave me some coins, and I bought a cake with a hole in it, called a doughnut. Everywhere people were bustling about dressed in the finest clothes. I had not seen so many stores, hotels, tea-houses, tailors, and a huge shop called a department store that seemed to sell everything. I remember Father noticed the rich golden hue of polished kauri on the drawer fronts of a Duchess in the window of a furniture store. It looked like salmon in the sunlight. Come and see, our sideboard in the sitting room is similar."

Maisy followed me to our dark sitting room with wood panelling half-way up the walls and red floral wallpaper above. A brass gas light hung from the ceiling.

"Isn't this your favourite corner, Phee, next to the bookshelf?"

"Yes, Hannah … an entire wall of glorious books and my favourite armchair. Father commissioned this suite to be made by your friend's uncle. He did the upholstery on the steamer *Waireka*. I like to run my hands on the beautiful wood trim and red fabric. This sideboard Father had made by a carpenter who worked on finishing the ship's cabins. He had found this glorious piece of heart kauri and offered to make it for Father. He cut pieces that mirrored each other on the cupboard fronts and drawer fronts. They looked like pieces of quilted salmon in the sun, swept with red knots, shimmering in the soft light.

"How do they get the salmon in there?"

If not for Hannah's serious face, I would have roared with laughter. "It is not real salmon fabric. The timber starts off with deep pit saw cuts. The more the craftsmen planes and smooths the timber, the more the colours show. Almost like looking into still water instead of rippled water."

"That is what makes each piece unique! Like you, Maisy, the more the Master Craftsman works on us, the more we start to glow and shine!"

Maggie had composed herself and came to see what we were discussing. She said, "Oh, it seems an age since I went on a trip to Melbourne or Sydney. I am feeling a little jealous that Barbara might get to go shopping again in Melbourne."

"Maggie, your turn will come again.

There was a knock on the door and Bess came running. I opened the door and a man dressed in a postal uniform had a letter for Father to sign. "Oh, I am sorry but Captain McQuarrie has just left."

"You can sign for it, Miss?"

"A registered letter from Australia? It looks important, see this red wax seal, Hannah?"

"I hope it's not more bad news for Father," said Maggie.

"Yes. What a pity it did not come yesterday!"

Perhaps that was why Father seemed to have the weight of the world on his shoulders. I just could not shake the uneasiness I felt for him. I wanted to deny it, but I knew there was something afoot that I could not fathom. Father had made many fortunes along the way, but it had taken unbelievable courage to keep going amidst this wrecking. The captain said, 'It is a matter of honour.' He said "Lassie, the way you do the little things is the way you do everything." I did not know who I could talk to about him and considered I might have to visit Uncle John. No one knew Father like him, except Barbara, of course. I would make a batch of scones and take them.

I went about cleaning up the house in a flurry, trying not to imagine what bad news might be festering in that letter. The more I tried not to think of it, the more I began to wonder.

"Hannah, come and put these dresses away! And I have told you not to let Bess on your bed."

Chapter 5

About the House

"Yoo-hoo! Is anyone home?"

I stuck my head out from the scullery to see Aunt Christine placing her bonnet on the hat stand by the door.

"Oh, Aunt, how lovely to see you!"

The girls came running in. It had now been two weeks since Father had left and my plan to visit Uncle John had got lost in all the business of the house.

"Good morning, Aunt!

"Oh, good morning, girls. Come here and let me hug you."

Both girls called out in unison and embraced Christine, one on each side.

"What are you two up to on this Saturday morning?"

"We have tidied our room, which was a disaster. Luckily Barbara was not here to see it. We found some of Mary's dolls clothes tucked under her bed, which we washed and have been playing with."

"Come, you have impeccable timing, Aunt – I have hot tea in the pot. Sit down and I will pour you one." The two girls went back to their room.

"Thank you, Phee. I just thought I would call past and see how you were doing. Where is Murdoch, my favourite young man? Is he working today?"

"No, he developed a cough after that rain a week back and

I sent him to bed."

"Is it serious?"

"I am hoping it is influenza, which is so common this time of year, but I have dosed him up and given him chicken soup. He has improved a little."

"You cannot be too careful. Many strong young men die every year of influenza."

"Aunt, I am almost frightened by it, as Barbara has been so strict about keeping our chests and necks covered!"

"Yes, yes, of course."

"I love young Maisy, but she can be headstrong. Getting her ready for church yesterday, Argh! – she may only be nine but acts like a young lady already. She is very bright and sees everything."

"I suppose that's having big sisters to copy. I remember the same thing with your Mother!"

"Really? Tell me about Mother!"

"Annie always had the hand-me-downs, being younger, and loved to dress up in our dresses and clothes. She was much more temperate though. Always dreamed of being a mother. I think she might say it was her greatest achievement, caring for you all." She spoke about her childhood and her own children being sick at times, sister Barbara's condition and Father at sea.

"I really do not have patience the way Mother did. Maisy seems always to be dressing up in her sister's clothes, then leaving them piled on the floor. The other day I caught her in Mother's room wearing her gold necklace, with her cheeks plastered with mother's red rouge. She had crawled into an evening dress and looked like a caterpillar in an oversized skin. It was a funny sight."

"Oh, my!" Aunt covered her mouth, trying not to laugh.

"She had gathered the frilly hem so she could release Mother's trapped white evening shoes, teetering while trying to twirl. It did look terribly funny and, if I had not been cross, I think I would have burst out laughing." Christine had the most hysterical laugh, and we roared with delight.

"Those are the moments you must treasure, Phee. Was it not Grandad who'd say, 'Take time to smell the flowers!'"

"I am sure that is why Mother loved her garden so much. If *she* were here, Maisy would be even more spirited than she already is."

"I am sure you are doing a fine job, Phee; the children seem happy."

"Dug and Ken are, of course, completely inseparable, flying about the house like a swarm. I said to them yesterday, 'Barbara would not let you away with that!' I am quite hopeless. All they need do is apologise and give me a hug and I cannot be cross."

"Phee, have you ever noticed how often they finish one another's sentences? It seems to be getting worse. Could it be them missing Barb? She said the twins could be demanding."

"Well, they certainly keep me on my toes. Several times Mrs Laird has called me into the school in response to their behaviour. Murdoch is just the opposite, gets on with life and says very little. If he does something, it is important."

"He is such a quiet young man; I love making him blush. I give him a kiss on the cheek whenever I drop in."

"Yes, he is a great support sharing a room with the twins. Actually, Aunt, I am thinking about clearing out Mary's room so Maggie can have her own. She is nearly sixteen."

"What a great idea!"

"How will I break it to Father?"

"Do not worry about that – leave the Captain to me. I'll tell him it was my idea."

"You are quite naughty, Aunt." We both laughed.

I was about to ask her about Father but the clock in the hall chimed two and Aunt Christine leapt to her feet.

"Goodness! I must be off!" She picked up her bonnet and woollen coat and gave me a tight hug.

"Thanks for the tea. Send one of those rascals over for an afternoon, Dugald perhaps. He can help me stack some firewood."

"I will. Thanks for coming by."

"It was my pleasure! Call by if you need something."

I waved goodbye and closed the door, leaning on it as I gathered my thoughts. "Maggie! Maggie!"

"Yes!"

She came from the bedroom, looking slightly gloomy. "What do you say … while Father's away we clear out Mary's old room? I think it is time. You need to have a room of your own instead of sharing with Hannah and me."

Maggie's face lit up "Can I! Oh, I have prayed for this day! How marvellous! What shall I do with her things?"

"Well, Father is going to be shocked when he comes home, so pack up her stuff nicely into tea chests. We can store it in the basement.

"Phee, I will leave a few of her bits and pieces to remind us. I am sure he will be happy after the initial shock."

"Well, your brave Aunt said to say it was her idea!"

"How exciting. I will start straight away!"

She threw her arms around me and, running down the hallway, shouted, "There are plenty of old tea chests in the cellar. I will get the boys to help me bring them up! Ken! Dugie! Come and help!"

I called after her. "Maggie, if you were a bird, you would be a Tui. A heavenly voice, glorious and strong!"

Murdoch appeared in the doorway with his hair standing on end. "Murdoch, how do you feel?"

"I feel much better after that sleep. I dreamt I was in heaven and there was singing all around me. Then I woke to Maggie's singing coming up through the floor vents under my room. I swear her singing is like her mood, up and down through the house," he said, laughing.

"Yes, she is mostly a delight and great with the boys. I have enjoyed secretly listening to her practising for the Christmas concert in a few months."

"Singing around the piano at night is a lovely sound at the end of the day. You would hear it, sister, if you did not fall asleep doing needlework in the lamplight."

He looked at me with a cheeky grin. "Oh, you had better check your meal next time I dish up. I mistake the caustic soda for salt sometimes!"

He burst out in laughter like a gun going off, coughing his way to a crescendo at the end.

"I can see you are feeling a little better; the colour has come back into your face. Anyway, Maggie is better company than you," I said, smiling. "Did you see, we have almost finished Mother's floor rug?"

"That is the one she had half-finished before she passed?"

"Yes. It seems like we are always searching for old clothes over the last few months to cut up for weaving thread. It will be a great surprise for Father when he returns."

Hannah came into the room. "Emmie, when will I get my own room." She plonked herself on the chair. "It's not fair!"

"Maisy, I am older than you, and I still share with the twins.

Come with me … let's go and help, rather than sitting here scowling." Murdoch picked her up and carried her off in the direction of the excited chatter.

I was exhausted as the sun went down. The fire had reduced to embers and I did not have the strength to stoke it again. I had read the same line in my book ten times and wondered why I persisted in staying up late. The next moment I awoke to Maggie's shouts.

Chapter 6

Back to School

"Phee! Phee! It is today! The 12th! You need to be up." She was standing over me in her school clothes.

"I must have slept in, being in a bed by myself for the first time." I rubbed my face and quickly rose. Twisting my hair into a bun in the mirror, I called out, "Maggie! Use the billows and throw a few logs in the range!"

"Okay. I will also go and feed the chooks and bring in the eggs." She hurried off.

The morning went quickly, and after getting the children ready for school, I rushed off to the Telegraph Office to send an update to Barbara in Thames.

I forced my back into the shelter of the cold leather seat of the carriage, clutched my snuggly white lamb's wool scarf to my neck as a defense against the bracing wind, and tried to relax. The scarf, rediscovered while clearing Mary's room she had made it for me in a school project. It was not pretty but was all the more precious now she had passed away. My hands were slightly clammy even with the salty breeze sweeping in from the north, blowing in over the Waitemata Harbour and carrying scents of burning coal, wet timber and hot steel from the port. It was always reassuring to see smoke billowing from the tall chimney at the ironworks.

"Miss McQuarrie, there's a shawl you can wrap around your

shoulders in the small leather trunk next to you if you wish."

"Thanks, Nicolai. It is rather chilly now those black clouds have crept over the sky."

The carriage bumped along the rough street, its steel wheels crunching into the soft gravel.

Nikolai carefully held back the sulky as we plummeted down the familiar steep hill toward beach road.

From the hill, I always followed the reclaimed harbour's progress as it was filled in by workman with horses and cart-loads of rocks. They moved about like ants, filling in the old beach, tipping loads of rocks brought in for the reclaimed shore.

"Maggie's a bright lass. Anything special happening at her school today?"

"Yes, young Maggie's teacher has asked me to speak to her history class. They are doing a project about the history of the shipbuilding industry here in Auckland."

"You're a brave woman, Miss. Nothing would scare me more than standing in front of a class of students, especially at that age."

"I must admit I am nervous. Nicolai, what made you come from Yugoslavia?"

"Oh, Miss, I got the fever. Went in search of those allusive yellow specks. Made more money as an expressman in the port over the last year than four years swinging a pick and shovel."

"I'd like to see it. Father has a ship-yard there in Thames."

"Promise me you won't. It is a frightful place for a young woman. Crawling with men from every hell hole. I tell you, they can have it: the mud, icy water, freezing nights, sore backs, and hunger. Give me Parnell any day. It is like its own special community up here with its sweeping views of the ships in the

Waitemata."

"I love to hear all the local gossip coming from the bustling dockyards and the latest news from abroad. It is literally carried in the wind on sails across the sea, right here to little Queen Street wharf."

We passed by a man whipping his horse. "Oh, Nikolai! See how that workman is treating that poor horse. The cartwheels must be stuck in the mud. He's bowed down with such a heavy load!"

"Under pressure, Miss, to get it done. I can remember only months back picking up passengers from here at Nicol's shipyards."

"I do hate cruelty, but it is strange only months ago this beach was full of boats – in fact, only ten years ago these were grassy hills that are now covered in houses!"

"Have you noticed time speeds by faster as you get older?"

"Yes, men can vote at my age, Nicolai."

He laughed. "Miss, if you have your way, you will be voting soon enough … soon enough! Your Father is in the thick of it! It must have been a sight alright to have seen the boom of 75! One of about forty shipbuilders in the Auckland region, is it any wonder they have had to expand?"

"Yes, the Captain thinks it cannot happen quick enough!"

"He is a driven man, your father. Expects nothing less of his men. I hear it in the harbour he is well respected by all. He has heart – you do not see that much anymore. It is all about pounds, shillings, pence and gold if you can find it." He chuckled to himself.

"That is terribly observant of you, Nicolai. He does genuinely care for each of his men, but he loathes inefficiency. He likes a man to be honest and take pride in his work. You must be impatient for the new wharf, Nicolai."

"Yes, Miss. It's hard enough transporting heavy ports and trunks from all these ships. Space has been in short supply for goods and imports long enough, not to mention ships that could not dock till they dug out the harbour. The new dockyards will make it easy for ship repairs and loading kauri bound for Australia."

As we passed by the guest house on Beach Road, two Maori were perched on a stray kauri log smoking a pipe. Only weeks ago their canoes were drawn up on the beach, and Nicol's were launching ships in the curve of the beach. Already it was a rock wall embankment that had realigned the new road and defined the new harbour.

We ducked beneath the arched steel columns of the 'train bridge to nowhere', as the locals call it. It awaited completion, eventually connecting to the port, which would one day join up to the harbour and bring goods in and out by rail. That day, it stood like a scarecrow in the middle of a paddock spanning right across the top of Nicol's old shipyards.

The familiar school building seemed to loom larger as we drew nearer. It was a testament to the priority of education when the settlers arrived. Nicolai delivered me right to the grand entrance in front of the school. I paid him and patted his horse before he trotted off. "Thanks, Nicolai."

"All the best, Miss!"

Mrs Laird had been standing with her hands clasped on the front steps to the main office as the sulky rolled up. She was a matronly woman, who, in her white blouse and a full-length dress, looked older than her years.

We had met acrimoniously a few times over the last few years in a combined effort to tame the twins. Once she had even separated the boys into different classes as a form of control. This, of course, made matters worse, and in the end, they agreed to behave with the threat of going back to separation.

Parnell School

"Good day, Mrs Laird."

"Good morning, Miss McQuarrie. Are you feeling prepared?"

"I thought I was, but now I'm not so sure," I said, smiling.

"You will be fine. Just take a deep breath, look them straight in the eyes and be yourself."

I followed her comfortable leather shoes and strong footsteps down the hall. It felt strange to be back here after so many years, like trying on an old favourite coat that had been grown out of, one that had long past had its day of fashion. As we drew nearer, I could hear excited chatter through the open door.

"Good morning, class … you may take your seats. This is Euphemia McQuarrie, Maggie's older sister.

"As you know, Euphemia is bringing a history lesson about her father, Captain Hector McQuarrie. Unfortunately, he had to put out to sea earlier than expected so could not be with us today. A few weeks ago, I was kindly disposed toward this article about Captain McQuarrie's business. I thought it would be interesting to look at a brief history of shipping in our city and its effect on our economy. These are two of many such articles praising Mr McQuarrie's skill, design and business acumen taken from the *Auckland Star*.

This smart schooner, Meg Merrilees, *is making some grand runs reflecting great credit upon her builder Mr H. McQuarrie who is celebrated for turning out some of the best sea boats and the fastest schooners here in Auckland.*

As showing what can be done by our shipwrights, should occasion demand Mr Hector McQuarrie of McQuarrie and McCallum the builders of so many well-known steamers and schooners of Mechanics Bay having undertaken the repairs of the barque Essex and this vessel requiring an entirely new stem it became a necessity to obtain the timber from our local forests. Mr McQuarrie left on Friday with his men and was back on the Sunday following with a log of pohutukawa partly shaped for working. Facts like these should be widely known."

"I will hand over to you now, Miss. We look forward to hearing what you have to share with us."

I had been looking about the room at the freckly white faces. The students were wearing smart uniforms with white starched shirts. Many of the boys had pudgy faces like boys get just before manhood. The wooden desks with cast iron legs were always arranged in precise rows of six across and five deep. The stained wood panelling would have made the room dark if it were not for the large windows. A few pictures hung around the room and warm coats were neatly hung on hooks in the corner. I felt thankful to walk toward the open fire beside the teachers' desk as my feet were cold.

"Thank you for your kind words and for the opportunity to speak to you today. Good morning, class."

"Good m-o-r-n-i-n-g, Miss Mc-Qu-a-rr-i-e!"

"I recognise quite a number of you in relation to either St Stephens, Knox church or your parent's shipping businesses. I have done my best to gather information from my father's history to share with you today.

"Please raise your hand if your parents came to New Zealand on a ship in about the last forty years."

The whole class raised their hands.

"Oh, all of you! … Class, if I wanted to go to Melbourne today, how would I get there and how long would it take? Yes, John."

"Miss, it would take about ten to twelve days and you could go by sailing ship or steamer."

"Which would you prefer, John?"

"I like the sailing ships, Miss. They are quiet, don't smell of coal and sometimes are faster with the right wind."

"Well-spoken! And ladies, if I needed a new pair of gloves

or shoes, where would they come from?"

"Yes, Rowena Rushbrook?"

The girl's smile beamed. "My mother's shop in Queen Street, Miss. Rushbrook and Sneddon – 2s 6d."

Everyone laughed, and I started to relax. "Good. That's right. And, Miss, the fabric?"

"Oh, I suppose that came by ship, or the gloves were already made in Melbourne."

"Well done. A lot of settlers come here thinking we are in the Antipodes. Perhaps this is a nice way of saying we cannot be a sophisticated colony because we are so remote. However, the shipping industry has played a vital role in connecting our distant colony to the rest of the world. Is it possible to move Australia closer to us? No, of course not, but the faster our ships go the closer Australia becomes. Most importantly, economically, we can trade our goods around the world.

"*Your* creative design, vitality and passion are needed! You are the first generation of New Zealanders. Who knows it could be some of you girls who will be designing the new ships or even engines of the future!"

Many of the boys laughed and looked about the classroom, thinking it was a joke.

"Many of your parents brought their skills from other colonies like Britain, Scotland and Nova Scotia. We all owe a great deal to all the highly skilled settlers that came bringing skills – lawyers, doctors, farmers, shipwrights and people with a passion to create a wonderful new colony.

"Some of your parents will be considered the founding fathers of Auckland.

"How many of you are already thinking about being apprenticed next year? … Mmm, eight of you.

"There is a strong chance you will have something to do with shipping — as rope makers, captains, steelworkers, sailmakers, timbermen, engineers, designers, carpenters, upholsterers and many more. Girls, I have always dreamed of running my own business. You do not have to just settle for being nurses, secretaries or shop assistants.

"Lloyds down the road produces the finest quality New Zealand flax ropes. One example in Parnell is nine inches thick. This means we do not need to import them from the Philippines, saving time and helping our own economy.

My father is busy creating large and small ships out of local raw materials produced right here. Many of the forty shipbuilders here are at the forefront of design, and many of our ships are sold all over the world. He employs many fine people in his three shipyards – perhaps some of you boys might end up there too."

Chapter 7

Hector McQuarrie

"Here is a brief background to my father's life. Perhaps it is similar to some of your parents.

"Who of you is of Scottish descent? Okay, then about three-quarters of you will attest to Scotland's fierce winds and rugged rocky shores.

"The Captain was born in Mull on the 27th of January 1825 and became an apprentice shipbuilder. There will be some of you here thinking of being apprenticed as a shipwright. I can see that's you!"

"Yes, Miss. Jimmy Evans, Miss. I have been out trimming the sails with me da – it's exhilarating, like harnessing a wild stallion!" Everyone laughed. "But I love watching the ships being built."

"I know exactly what you mean. I love watching a ship come to life too!

"Father sailed in 1859, hearing stories on the wind of a gold rush in Victoria and searching for a better life for his family. The Captain was thirty-five and had also heard rumours Sir George Gray had helped a large Scottish highland community take up land in New Zealand.

"He set off for New Zealand after his wife, Margaret, died, and his daughter, Mary, to look after his parents, and to work his passage aboard a ship …

"… like you, Jimmy … my father was on the seas since he was a young boy, fishing and travelling around their small island. He survived many a terrific beating at sea, pitting his wits against the elements. He would say, 'The sea is the master and has the final word. That and God!'"

The children laughed.

"Many of the experiences we endure prepare us to be strong when life's many trials blow our way. Maggie will agree, our father has a thousand stories of adventures at sea. There is nothing more exciting for us than sitting around after supper, listening to his many sailor's tales. I hope this story in particular will be an interesting insight into our early history of Auckland and its economic struggle."

I took a deep breath and looked at the many keen eyes. The sun streaming through the windows and over my feet finally begin to warm them up.

"The Captain needed four things for success. What do you think they might be?"

"Catherine, Miss … timber!"

"Yes good … over there, Peter!"

"Finances and a shipyard!"

"Good!"

"Maggie."

"A wife!?"

We all laughed. "Well done, yes! A plentiful supply of just the right timber, skilled craftsmen, a yard, harbour and don't forget plenty of courage.

"As he sailed up the coast from Auckland, he found the most perfect little harbour in Little Omaha with a plentiful supply of just the right timber. Kauri. Many Nova Scotians were skilled shipwrights as Nova Scotia also had a plentiful supply of good timber and they built hundreds of ships. They settled in Waipu and Leigh, among the kauri forests and immediately got to work building.

"Father bought a small cottage from a Maori family about to burn it down, as their son had died in it. He built a raft and floated it to McQuarrie's Flat where it still stands today as a local public house called *The Jolly Fisherman*.

"Has anyone been to Leigh? Oh, … most of you!

"You may have seen *The Jolly Fisherman's* bar in Little Omaha harbour?"

A few children nodded.

"He built a sawmill beside McQuarrie's Flat, in the creek using the power of the water to drive the blades. The massive logs for the mill were rolled down the hills and off the cliffs into the sea. They also built massive dams in the streams, felled the trees into the valleys, and then let the dams go, washing the trees into the sea where they barged them to the mill.

"After a few years, he met my mother in Auckland, Annie McCleod, who had also settled from Nova Scotia in 1856. They were married, and Father's first ship was launched in 1865 called the *Banshee*. I love this name as Father would sometimes say 'She's howling like a Banshee.'

"There were many highlanders in the settlements that not only shared the same Gaelic language but the same spirit. Father became good friends with many of the men that were a strong influence in establishing Auckland, men like Captain McKenzie, Captain Fraser, John McGregor, Captain McLeod.

"He met Duncan Matheson who had brought out the last of the seven ships of Nova Scotian settlers. They bought the *Spray*, refitted her in Nova Scotia and carried the last thirteen families to Leigh in 1857 ... 99 passengers in all.

"What materials do you think these early settlers might have used on their house rooves?"

"Wooden shingles, Miss?"

"Yes, but initially they used grass thatching. When you think of it, it is quite unbelievable what has been achieved in forty years in this colony, isn't it? It was hard work and many folk arrived expecting it to be a modern city. In 1867 the colony was struggling with unemployment.

"10,000 British soldiers, who were stationed in New Zealand, were ordered to return to Britain. Many thought they were taking with them the people's hopes and dreams of a great colony. The soldiers sold up and took their pay back with them in English pounds which created a shortage of notes and coins on the street. The colony was fragile, and this helped tip the balance, driving the economy into a desperate state.

"People petitioned the government to do something as some by now were starving.

"They created a flax industry, gum-digging, rock-breaking and even a coal mine in The Waikato, which all eventually petered out.

"Here are a couple of quotes from people who were here at the time.

"The reform league met and decided the best thing the whites could do is to get out of the country and go to another place with greater prosperity."

"They filled the barracks and immigration quarters with the unemployed and their dependents and set up a soup kitchen. To what better use could they be put - there will be no more immigrants come here!"

"Mr Quartier, a wealthy jeweller, saw an opportunity to make some money and offered passengers a way of escape to America.

"He commissioned Father to build the first ship sailing directly to San Francisco. No expense was spared and by the time it was finished, the passengers were desperate to board and leave the colony. In this economy, Father launched his second ship called the *Flying Cloud*.

"However, for the captain, storms were brewing of a different kind, perhaps his greatest in thirty-six years.

Hector McQuarrie

Chapter 8

Flying Cloud Debacle

"Your parents will probably remember only too well the debacle of April 67 … This was three years before I was born, yet still today, twenty-six years later, people ask me if I'm related to Hector McQuarrie of the *Flying Cloud*. This is a story that has it all … adventure, piracy, unexplained death, swindlers, intrigue, gold, and injustice. Girls, I am sorry, there's no romance." A small chuckle rippled around the room.

"The name was chosen from another American ship launched in 1851. She still has an unbroken world record for the fastest run between New York and San Francisco, of eighty-nine days.

"The two ships were about to duel in San Francisco Bay, like David and Goliath. Have any of you been on a ship where the captain is trying to race another boat?"

"Yes, Miss, it's exciting!" some of the boys called out.

"A beautiful, sleek 300-ton vessel built to conquer the seas at breakneck speed, she was built with some of the finest materials in the world.

"Here is a picture I took off Father's office wall. Perhaps you could pass it around.

"When you see the rugged harbour of Little Omaha, now called Leigh, it is incredible to imagine a massive ship being built there.

Little Omaha Harbour

"Has anyone called into that harbour on a journey north?" Many hands went up. "Yes, many of you."

"I would love to have seen my father's face the first time he fully set the three masts of the *Frank Guy*, as he sailed out on the 28th of March. It was one of the first ships wholly built from local New Zealand materials – kauri and pohutukawa, sails and flax ropes, steel anchors, winches and ironworks.

"Sarah, your parents' business, Fraser & Tinne, is making a

huge impact in the shipping industry from here in Auckland.

"Everyone agreed it was a fine-looking vessel, and perhaps this was the ship father had dreamed of one day building. He was so proud of the efforts of the whole community in Little Omaha. To celebrate, he offered free passage to Auckland Harbour to anyone wanting to come along for the ride. Thirty-two people boarded for its maiden voyage back down the coast to the Queen Street jetty. Perhaps there was even folk on board who were leaving for California.

"Here is another quote from someone in those days:

"… strong inducements were held out to the would-be deserters of Auckland to rake together their last pence for passage money to get away to "The Land of Gold …"

"As the captain set about preparing to leave Little Omaha that day he was focused on another kind of build, but this time not in a shipyard. Any ideas?"

"A house, Miss?"

"Good, Miss Foster! He had promised Annie, my mother, a fine new home on the cliffs in Parnell overlooking the harbour, only walking distance to the new shipyard in Mechanics Bay.

"They were expecting my oldest sister, Barbara, their first. He had put everything into this ship to make enough to build a home for their first bairn. He just needed Mr Quartier to pay what was owing.

"Mr A. Quartier, at thirty-five years old, was already a prominent society figure. He had a glorious property, walking distance to the city, and other shipping interests. The *Flying Cloud* would be his as soon as the outstanding funds were paid, and the completion certificate signed.

"The disgruntled settlers had been hearing many rumours from California – *there is gold in the streets*. In a few days, the would-be deserters would be setting sail, once all the food and stores were loaded on board for the long journey. However, things were about to get a little more complicated.

The Flying Cloud

"The ship was delivered, and, on the 3rd of April, the only thing needed to complete the purchase was a Bank cheque.

"As many as 150 settlers had now paid £12 to escape on 6th of April and boarded the ship for the *Land of Gold*. Most had sold all their possessions, property and goods just to pay for their fare. Mr Whooley had advertised fares till the last minute and had approximately £1,500, the total value of the ship, when word got out there would be delays.

"By now all the passengers were on board and cleared by customs. What were they to do?

"Mr Quartier was arranging his final payment to Father but did not have enough cleared funds in his account. He suggested four things to speed up the process: If Mr McQuarrie would accept a post-dated cheque, dated a few days from now … the Bank of Auckland manager could sign it to guarantee payment. Mr McQuarrie could proceed to sign the builder's certificate, and the ship would then be his and could be cleared to leave.

"They could all set sail and be on their way on the first of many voyages to America.

"Here is another quote from a young Aucklander at the time:

In a short time, the brig's accommodation was filled, and passengers were regarded by those they were leaving behind, to be the luckiest fellows alive

…

"The luckiest fellows alive … Class, isn't it interesting that we can often look at someone's situation and think "They are so lucky, I wish that had been me!" Then a little time goes by and we are so happy it wasn't us!

"They had a *secret*, class! What do you think it was? … Yes?"

A young man at the back with vibrant red hair raised his hand.

"Mark McIntosh, isn't it? I think you delivered firewood to our house last month with your older brother."

"Yes, Miss! … Mr Quartier was bankrupt!"

"Well done! How did you know that?"

"My cousin was eighteen at the time and was leaving to make his fortune. He never got his money back, but while he was stuck on the ship, they discovered gold here in Thames. He made enough in three years to buy land."

"So, in some ways, Mark, he might have been the lucky one after all!

"The Bank manager, Mr Johns, was more than happy to sign the post-dated cheque, for he also secretly had personal interests in profiting from the *Flying Cloud's* departure.

"However, things were not as they seemed, and only the Bank Manager and Mr Quartier knew there was no money forthcoming. Mr Auriel Quartier, as you said, Mark, was bankrupt and owed a fortune of £8,000 to many folk.

"Unbeknown to Hector, the bank had already dishonoured many cheques of Mr Quartiers that week. Perhaps they hoped that within a day or so they would be on the fastest ship to California, and who could stop them?

"The passengers on the ship were in high spirits because either tomorrow or at least by the next day they would be off. One day dragged into another until word got out that the boat would not be leaving.

"Most folk had absolutely nowhere to go, having sold everything, so the anchors stayed down, and the passengers began to eat the provisions on board. One month turned into two and three.

"Rowena, has anyone in your mother's shop left without paying?"

"Yes, Miss. Quite a few times."

"How do you think your mother felt?"

"She took it rather personally, and said, 'Why would they do that to me!' It has made her lose trust and faith in people."

"This is the feeling that both Aucklanders felt toward the passengers and the passengers felt toward the colony. The people of Auckland began by feeling jealous of those leaving and did not feel sympathetic to their plight at all. Many who were leaving on the ship had spoken of their joy at leaving the colony. People viewed them like rats escaping a burning ship. However, slowly their joy at leaving turned to shame as they realised that each day the ship seemed less and less likely to leave.

"The people of Auckland felt they had gotten what they deserved. Now the deserters would have to eat humble pie and ask for food and support from the colony they had been so happy to desert. Now they were looking for someone to blame!"

I took my shawl off the back of my chair and wrapped it around my shoulders. Even though the fire was right beside me, next to the blackboard, it was a sizable room and the fire was creating a draft.

"They started to get desperate and petitioned the ticket office, who had taken their £1,500 in fares to return it. They petitioned the local police as well, as they had been robbed.

"They tried to reason with the ship's owner, Mr Quartier, and the bank, then entreated the politicians and said the government should step in, then the council, and harbour board for not letting the ship leave. Then they beseeched the courts, but no case had yet been tried like it in New Zealand. It fell between Maritime law, English law and New Zealand law.

"They tried to blame my father.

"Finally, they begged the Governor of New Zealand, Sir George Gray, to step in. All to no avail. This complex case would be destined for the High Court."

Chapter 9

Piracy and Gold

Mrs Laird quietly spoke to one of the boys, who made his way between the desks to the front. Excusing himself, he chose a few logs from the wood box and carried them to the hearth. Using the poker to stir up the coals, the boy placed the wood on the fire.

"Thank you, young man."

The children were intrigued by the story and settled again quickly.

"It was an irony, the only people who could help the squatter's plight was the colony they gladly planned on leaving. They had no choice but to beg for charity. Though the colonists were in desperate times, they humbled themselves and gave what they could to help.

"One businessman arranged a grand theatrical event in his theatre and then gave all the proceeds to help the passengers' misery.

"How do you think you would feel? Have any of you had times when your parents had no food in the house? " Some children wriggled nervously.

"Yes, Miss. Mary, Miss. My father picked grass off the side of the road to feed people's horses to make enough to buy potatoes for us."

"Thank you for sharing that! Your father is a resourceful

man. Anyone else? … Yes, Mary."

"How did your Father feel?"

"That is a great question. I am not actually sure. I think he put his faith in God and the law courts, hoping for justice.

"The *Flying Cloud* became famous. Stories were plastered daily across every newspaper in New Zealand about the conditions of those on board, laying blame back and forwards for four months on end.

"The passengers were desperate, and next they plotted Piracy! Twice secret plots were hatched by the passengers to pirate the ship in the dead of night.

"A French captain was smuggled on board with plans to slip silently away in the middle of the night. The acting Captain Seon got wind of this villainous scheme and with the police made haste to the ship in the dark. They quickly crossed over the harbour and boarded the *Flying Cloud*, swiftly apprehending the perpetrators.

"A few days later, an *Auckland Star* reader suggested they remove the sails to prevent any further treachery.

"On the 6th of May, an article was printed by those on board in the harbour, laying the full blame squarely at the feet of both the bankrupt Mr Quartier and the infamous Bank manager who by now had absconded.

"They stated, *"what a disgraceful act of fraud had been done to the shame of the whole colony of New Zealand.*

"The pressure of the scandal and Mr Quartier's shame became too much. The newspapers refused to print any more articles of the dramas aboard, and Mr Quartier was found dead."

There was a sudden gasp from the room and lots of surprised faces and murmurings hummed.

"No one quite knows what happened to the young Mr Auriel Quartier. Within forty-eight hours, he mysteriously passed away."

Mrs Laird rose to her feet. "Now, class, please be quiet for Miss McQuarrie."

"On the 9th of May, the flag on board was reluctantly flown at half-mast by the passengers on board. As Mr Quartier was laid to rest, the passengers could feel black clouds and a storm of a different kind brewing. Auriel was free but not the passengers or the debt."

For those in government, what do you think this whole affair highlighted? … Yes, Peter."

"Do something to stop people leaving the new colony for gold in California or gold in Victoria!"

"Yes, well done … the young lady with long plaited hair! Oh, it is you, Sarah."

"That something drastic must be done to help those on board, Miss."

"Well done, everyone. What incredible insight! Yes, at that time, people were leaving the colony in droves to go to Australia and on other ships to America. On top of that, with all the soldiers leaving, the colonists were afraid of further uprisings breaking out with the Maoris. Even the government appeared to be broke. Here is a circular in 1867 to the head of departments under the Provincial Government requesting they notify their subordinates.

"no funds are available for their salaries for another year and that their services will be dispensed of."

The Provincial Government were desperate to reverse the outgoing tide of people leaving for California and Australia.

"Peter, what would you do if you were in government?"

"Create a gold rush, Miss."

"For what reason?"

"It would reverse the flow of people leaving the colony. It would stimulate the economy and bring new migrants and new settlers into New Zealand."

"Well done, Peter Fraser. You could be running the country one day! That is exactly what happened. On the 26th of April 1867 Mr John Williamson, as superintendent of the province, offered the largest reward ever to anyone finding gold leading to new fields being opened in the Auckland region.

"Who can guess how much? Yes, Miss Craig."

"£1,000, Miss?"

"Good guess, but it was five times that amount – £5,000."

"Wow!!!" The whole class were astonished.

"Okay, class, settle down. You can ask questions soon," said Mrs Laird.

Many of the students had been leaning in, and now especially the boys were squirming to say something. "Obviously, many of you have stories about the gold in Thames … Perhaps I could hear from two people. Yes, over there!"

"Gael McLeod, Miss. My father discovered gold up in Kennedy's Bay in 1868. And he discovered the Tokatea reef with good gold. He applied for a portion of the reward but was denied as it was already in the region of the Coromandel and Kennedys, not the Auckland region."

"That is a great story. How wonderful for your family. I know there will be many others, but I will just take one more. Yes, Master McGregor!"

"My father was living in the Coromandel for about fifteen

years at the time of the reward, working for gold, He turned a ship around in Thames, making haste to lay a claim to it. Mr Ring boarded with him for Auckland, but even though Father was paying his lodgings, Mr Ring was awarded £200. He received it because they took into consideration that, from 1852, Coromandel had already been a productive goldfield. Father received nothing."

"I am sorry to hear that, but at the time, people came out of the woodwork like ants from a nest to make claims. Some fraudulently brought gold from elsewhere and tried to fake a fresh strike."

"Here is another quote:

"In July of that year it was reported that a block of Land on the Thames River, about 55 miles from Auckland, had been discovered to be "Full of Gold". Prior to this a native chief Taipari from Ohinemuri, claimed the reward for his tribe. Further investigation resulted in the proclamation and opening of the goldfield.

"Do you wonder what folk on the *Flying Cloud* thought of all this?

"The Bank of Auckland illegally kept possession of the *Flying Cloud* as security over Mr Quartiers debt, while on the other hand, maintaining the bank manager, Mr Johns had no authority to clear the cheque. Sadly for Father, neither the half share of the ship was returned to Father or his half of the money.

"Father waited for six months for the court case, thinking an honourable judge in the Supreme Court would bring swift justice to the Bank. However, it was nothing short of robbery.

After weeks of hearings, a jury ruled unanimously in Father's favour. Unfortunately, the judge overturned the verdict of the entire jury and voted in favour of the Bank.

"The New Zealand public had heard enough and hundreds of articles were published over the following five months. Finally, on the 28th of August, everyone was removed from the ship. Two days later it was sold at auction for £1,950 and the money given to the Bank who also had the £1,500 from the sale of the tickets. It set sail a week later, on the 5th of September with seventy passengers on board bound for Sydney on its maiden, open sea voyage.

"I chose this story because I believe that the *Flying Cloud* debacle was a turning point for New Zealand and a catalyst for politicians to wake up and do something quickly! I believe the shame over the *Flying Cloud* caused the government to drastically rethink ideas economically, reversing the flow of people leaving New Zealand.

"It has been said that 'Auckland was Built on Thames'. Rumours of a gold rush spread like fire, and gold seekers poured back into New Zealand from all over the world. Thames' population swelled to more than Auckland's. Within a few years, I imagine all the destitute folk who had been on board the *Flying Cloud* are today enjoying the prosperity of Auckland. Perhaps they were in fact 'the luckiest fellows alive'.

"I have a few minutes for questions."

Many hands shot up, and I suddenly felt quite weary, and my mouth was dry. "Yes, Casey."

"Miss McQuarrie, did your Father ever get paid?"

"Months later, the Bank offered him a deal that he had no choice but to accept. Although I do not know what settlement he took. He had made his peace with God and was rewarded by a miracle.

"Just before Christmas of that year, he and five other Nova Scotian men had formed a syndicate together which struck gold and made them all a small fortune."

"Miss, what happened to all the people off the boat?"

"Some that had enough money bought another ticket and sailed off to California only weeks later, but most, however, would have had to stay and find work. As you have probably read, within three years, Auckland was booming. Yes?"

"Luke, Miss. Did your Father really build the first tugboat for the Northern Steam Ship Company with duel engines and 300 horsepower? And did he build many boats for the Northern Steamship Company?"

"Yes, Luke. The *Awhina* did a lot of work in this harbour for the people of Auckland. She has been a powerful steamer for her time; she was sold a few years back into Fremantle, Western Australia. But she towed ships in or out of the harbour, dragged ships off reefs or those gone ashore on beaches and sand bars. He built quite a few boats for them – I am not sure how many.

"Yes, over in the back corner!"

"Simon, Miss. You said there were pirates … did anyone get shot when they took over the boat?"

I couldn't help laughing. "No, Simon, but I think there could have been a few people who would like to have shot each other.

"I will have to leave the questions now because I will finish before lunch with a piece my father wrote. It is called Banshee.

Banshee

Black clouds loom in the night,
Fierce winds lashing the deck
Each cold blast threatening life,
Buried under crushing waves,

Desperate breath, neath sheets of white,
One on another, score upon score,
Man the pumps boys least we go under
Drowning our hope, dreams, will to fight,
Morning light rises, visiting once more,
Fear subsides, seas calm at the Helm,
Cast off lad, trim the sails, steer her course,
Now we are stronger than before.

"Class, I would like to leave you with a few thoughts today!

"Experiences that we endure in life shape who we are and give us the courage God intended us to show, even though at the time they may seem crushing. He is witness to our kindness and it should be a currency of gold we never cease giving to others.

"Thank you, class, for your participation – you have shown great insight. I have enjoyed being with you all today."

Mrs Laird thanked me, and one of the boys handed me a painting they had done of the *Flying Cloud*.

Mrs Laird walked out with me, encouraging me to consider teaching. She said she would like to have me come again.

I walked home, up and over the hill, and could not wait to take off my shoes. I did not know how Barbara managed on her feet all day.

It was warm and quiet on the porch, and I slipped off my shoes and rubbed my feet, thinking how much I would look forward to a bath that night. I browsed the pages of the *Auckland Star* to relax a little. It was already past lunchtime, and I tried not to think about dinner. I glanced at the classified ads to take my mind off the classroom when I saw a most curious advertisement amongst the clothing ads.

I checked the date again: 17th July 1893. It appeared by a Mrs

François Vine. It read "This is to notify that the ownership of the *Frank Guy* is in dispute."

What does that mean? Who is Mrs Vine?

Chapter 10

Tested with Fire

I had been pondering about Mrs Vine all afternoon. Was she an investor? I could only imagine that the sealed letter from Australia had something to do with her and was tempted to take a hot iron and melt the wax to read it. My day had disappeared in a blur with this curious affair! But I was suddenly distracted by the orange light filling the lounge with a bright glow! Looking out towards the heads, there was a glorious sunset across the sea. Orange and red fire reflected in the still harbour.

"Children, come quick!" I could hear a mad scramble throughout the house as the children and the dog came running and barking.

"Is it Father?" Ken jumped up to see over the rail.

"No, I'm not expecting him for a while, but look at the magnificent sunset!!"

Ken looked quite deflated "Oh, is that all."

Murdoch came and hung himself over Ken like a coat rack.

"It's on fire!" Hannah exclaimed excitedly.

"It reminds me of the night of the fire at the shipyard. I was only about your age, seven."

"I'm not seven, I'm nine!" Hannah said indignantly.

I reached out and took her hand. "Yes, of course you are, but I still remember waking in the dark to excited voices, and running about the house. I stood frozen on the balcony looking down over the bay through Mother's warm legs."

The children's interest was stirred at the sound of a story. "I remember orange flames and embers dancing up into the dark night. The sea looked like it was on fire, reflected just like tonight."

Dug was deep in thought as he asked, "How did it start?"

"Father had ship blocks stacked in the shipyard against the wall of Fraser & Tinne's next door. They had caught alight and were about to set the ship on fire that was sitting on stocks."

Maggie spoke up quite suddenly, sounding almost like a news reporter. "It started from wooden nails that we dry at night on top of the furnace at the foundry next door. This makes them hard so they can be hammered into planks on the ships. The furnace must have been too hot when they were placed in there, which caused them to catch alight."

Shipyard at Mechanics Bay. Hull under construction

"My, I think you would make a great woman detective or reporter. How do you know that, Maggie?"

"We have learned a great deal about shipping with our history lessons at school."

"You could not be a detective – you would hate to get your shoes dirty!" Dug scoffed

Maggie punched his arm. "Dug, you can be mean sometimes."

"That is enough! Do you want to hear the rest of the story?"

Dug folded his arms. "Yes!"

"I remember Father had invited our neighbours, Mr and Mrs Peters, over for a special dinner to thank them for their bravery. His quick thinking saved many people's livelihood."

"I like Mr Peters. He sometimes throws a ball with me when father is away. What did he do to help?"

"He was on watch that night at the Sash and Door company and saw the flames at Fraser & Tinne. Back and forth he ran with buckets until others joined in and they had the fire under control. It took a while for the repairs to be finished, but even the fire siren in Parnell got fixed."

I crouched slightly, teasing Hannah "There's a whole bowl of boiled lollies on the table."

"Oh please, please, Emmie?"

"Alright, Hannah. Murdoch, can you reach the glass jar of lollies?"

Ken was looking intently. "Phee, there is a tiny sliver of moon! It looks like a smile!"

"Mother would always say 'It is holding up the rain', like a bowl," Maggie said.

Turning his head, Ken looked up. "What? Oh, I can see that now!"

"Do you know why Father invited the Peters over to say thank you? Because there was another fire when I was not even born that Father saved the whole city from!”

“What! How?”

“It was just down here in Official Bay, as it was called then. I found the article Mother had cut out and placed in her journal.

“Someone had built a large fire in the bay, but there was a strong wind blowing embers into the air from the east. The buildings were all built of timber and had wooden shingles on the roof. There were many buildings there, including tenement houses, the post office and other government buildings. Father saw that one had caught on fire and, without hesitation, scrambled up on the roof and vigorously pulled tiles off to save it. Looking from there, he could see other fires starting behind the Belfast Hotel in dry grass near a vacant house. The fire was well underway on the house veranda, so Father ripped up the boards that were on fire and doused the flames in buckets of water.

“The newspaper praised Father’s energy and promptitude, saying he had stopped what would have been one of the greatest fires ever seen in Auckland. That is why we have fire sirens throughout the city now.”

“Did he get a reward?

“No, Ken, but a family in the area asked him to dinner to say thank you.”

“Tell us again about the fire here, Phee!”

I smiled and looked toward Ken. “I do not think I can remember another fire. Perhaps Ken might remember it better. It wasn’t long after the shipyard fire!”

“Oh, I don’t think I want to remember this one!”

“Well, children, it is actually just as well that the siren in Parnell had been fixed because Father got fined five shillings —

about half a week's wages. Perhaps you would you like to tell the story, Ken."

"I will, I will!"

"No, Dug, let your brother."

"Murdoch, I had not really noticed your trousers are short on the legs! I did not realise you had grown that much!

"His voice is breaking!"

"Maggie!" Ken had a look on his face just like Father's.

"Sorry, Ken, go on with the story."

"How can you break your voice?"

"Quiet, Maisy, it's Ken's turn to speak."

"Are you sure you want to hear this?"

"Yes!" We all called out in unison.

"Well, Dug and I came home asking for any old newspapers. Our friends at school had told us you can get whole pieces to fly up into the night sky, if you get the fire big enough! We scrunched up old papers then stuffed them in the fire and set them alight. It was so exciting. We were running outside to look at them flying up out into the night sky then floating back down with embers glowing round the edges of each piece. Suddenly, there was a huge whoosh! and a loud cracking in the roof. Flames were leaping out the chimney as tall as me. The paper had burned with such fury, it had set the residue coke inside the chimney on fire. Father heard the noise and managed to scramble onto the roof with water and put it out.

"Mother had been asking Father to get the chimney sweep in for months. He told us the story about him saving the houses."

"Yes, that's right, Ken! And, Dug, what was your punishment?"

"Father made us chop firewood for a week after school and

stack it in the woodshed."

"You were lucky it didn't spread to the roof timbers or we would have no woodshed or house to live in." Murdoch had returned with the lollies and shared them around.

"She got two!" Dug said accusingly.

"Hannah, put it back."

"I remember the fire warden came asking questions about the chimney fire. I told him it was not me!" Murdoch looked so innocent.

Hannah now had one big lump in each cheek, having popped two in her mouth before anyone could stop her. She looked at me with her innocent, princess face.

"You can each have another one, except Maisy."

We snuggled in on the bench seat and Maggie wrapped us in a blanket while Bess jumped up on our laps.

"Oh, you are so heavy," Maggie said. "I wish Father and Barbara were here!"

The sky was almost purple now, and Venus was bright. Murdoch stoked the fire up and the light danced about on the walls. "Play something for us, Phee," said Murdoch.

I strolled to the piano, and lifted the walnut lid. "Come on, Maggie, lead us in a chorus." While Maggie led us in the singing, there was an air of contentment as we later went off to bed. I had forgotten completely about Mrs Vine for a few hours.

Chapter 11

Scones with Uncle John

I woke early to thoughts of Mrs Vine and decided to keep busy with a few chores. "Good morning, Maggie, you look lovely. I've got leftover eggs from the boys if you want one?" She was dressed in a long pink dress and had her hair tied back in a bun.

"No, thanks. Tabitha Craig is coming over. I want to practise that piece *Canary Birds* for the Mission Social."

"Oh, lovely. Hannah and I are making scones that I will take down to Uncle John. Can you keep an eye on her while I am away?" I had decided to ask Uncle John for an opportunity to train in office management!

"She's no trouble; she's working on a piece of embroidery that Eileen started with her."

"Bother! I just remembered I used the last of the flour a few nights ago making Yorkshire puddings when Mr and Mrs Kelly came for supper," I muttered to myself as Maggie played and hummed her piece to warm up her voice. The range was still hot and a great way to keep the house warm on an overcast wintery day. I threw another shovel of coal in the fire and removed my apron. I shouted out to Hannah, who was probably dressing up her favourite china doll that Mother had given her for her fifth birthday. "Hannah, I am just going to get flour at the corner grocer." As I came onto the street, my neighbour was passing.

"Morning, Pheemie, how are you? Any word from the Captain?"

"Good morning, Mrs Peters. Nothing yet! I am keeping busy around the house, and I am not really expecting him for a few more weeks. I was about to make a few scones with Hannah, but we're out of flour."

"I can spare you 'alf a pound of flour!"

"Thank you kindly, but I need to get out of the house!"

"Well then, deary, they've got fresh Canterbury flour down on the corner today."

I thanked her and called Bessy. "Come on, girl, let's go for a walk." We had acquired Bessy as a wee ball of fluff when Mary got sick; she was the cutest black spaniel puppy. She used to sleep on Mary's bed, much to Father's disgust.

"Morning, Bella!" The Italian family up the road had two daughters that ran out to pat Bess whenever they see us. Bella ran across the street and patted Bessy, who wagged her whole body with excitement.

"Good girl. *Good* girl."

"Bella, I'm just going to the store. Would you like to have her? You could bring her by the house later!"

"Oh, can I!?"

Bess was such great company when there was no one about. She jumped on our bed in the morning when it was barely daylight. I would scold her as she was not allowed, but it didn't stop her. She would sometimes randomly bury her nose into my knee when she sensed I felt more like the day, a little overcast and cloudy.

I returned home, and Hannah and I set about getting the few ingredients out for the scones. I had some nice hot coals in the firebox, so I swung open the cast iron door and threw in a few smaller logs.

"Phee, did you cook in the kitchen with Mother?"

"Yes, I loved cooking with Mother. It was my favourite thing when there was only the two of us in the house. Barbara was still teaching then. Mother showed me how to master the art of keeping the oven at just the right temperature to bake and not burn everything."

"Can you show me too?"

"Okay. This is how we keep the oven at just the right heat. Once there is a good bed of hot coals, we take these smaller pieces that the boys have chopped and just put a little more in every now and then. This helps regulate the heat."

"I see. It is like putting on your hat or taking it off?"

"I hadn't thought of it that way, but I suppose you're right." Hannah was rolling up a ball of dough she had made from the left-over flour and then popped it in her mouth.

"Do you think they will be done yet?" Maggie said.

"What does the clock say?" She danced to the clock and stood looking at it on the mantle-piece.

"It's been nine minutes so far! Can I wind the clock?"

She ran and fetched a chair and quickly stood on it in front of the fireplace. "Just be careful. Once you have done that, we will get the scones out, we don't want them to burn." I carefully snuck a peek – they had risen beautifully. Hannah returned the chair and skipped back like a dancer.

"Careful! They are hot!"

She took the cloth and together we brought them out of the oven and placed them on the cooling tray.

"They smell so good! Can I have one now?"

"There's fresh butter I made this morning in the safe." I proudly wrapped a handful of scones in a cloth. I think the fresh flour made them rise better.

"Scones! Can we have some, Phee?" The boys came rushing in.

"I swear you boys are continuously hungry, especially you, Murdoch. Help yourself, boys. I will be home later."

I carried the warm scones to my chest, walking briskly down the hill to the end of Augustus Terrace. The view of the shipyards was spectacular from the long set of stairs that led to a path over the railway line. It was less than a mile to the office from there.

I could already see the huge ribs of a new ship in the stocks. The beautiful fragrance of the pohutukawa and kauri logs wafted past as I made my way closer. Two men swinging an adze shaved great hunks of wood off a rib to square it off. A group of men laid boards straight from the hot box onto a small hull. Old Bashin swung a huge hammer like a toothpick, his muscles the size of oars as he hammered the copper nails into the lapping boards.

"Good morning!" A few men fitting cross beams on the deck stopped work and waved as I passed by the scaffolding, carefully placing my feet so not to trip. It was a man's world down here. Even with equal rights, I would never attempt to swing that huge hammer. I glanced up for a second as a young man crawled out from under the hull. My heart immediately soared into my mouth and I started to feel a little faint. I stood and stared for what seemed like an eternity. He was wearing shorts with braces clipped to them. They almost framed his strong bare chest. His muscly legs bulged a little as he stood up and turned toward me.

"Euphemia, good morning!"

My voice froze, and my tongue turned dry. *What do I say?*

Could he know of the dream I'd had? I smiled and pretended to concentrate again on my feet. He was in Father's old gang; the Captain is not officially building ships here now, but he keeps his office here and McGregor's use the yard for small projects.

Thankfully, Mr McGrath called out. "Morning, lassie. How's your family? I believe you are the mother of the house! They are blessed to have you!"

Old Mr McGrath was always lovely and sometimes, scolded the men for calling out.

"They are all well, thank you for asking. How is your Beatrice?"

"She's well too, lassie! I will let her know you asked."

I glanced back to catch sight of Duncan as I entered the corridor, but he was gone. I always thought it was like stepping into another world away from the noise of hammers and saws, felt strange to walk past Father's office. I wanted to pop through the door and see him sitting there.

I stood for a second at the six-panel kauri door, the shiny brass plaque reading, JOHN MCCALLUM. I knocked and called out "It's just me!" John looked up from his desk and his face suddenly lit up.

"Phemie! How are ye, lassie? You gave me such a fright. I thought I was hearing a ghost, you sound so like your mother. Look at ye! … looking more pretty every time I see ye."

"I am well, thank you." I gave him a little hug and turned to look about the room. It had been a while since I had been here. It was a beautiful room with dark wood panelling and red velvet chairs, the fabric left over from the men's quarters of the glorious steamer *MacGregor*. Uncle John was really my first cousin. He had Granny's brilliance for numbers and was a born salesman. They were involved in mining phosphate."

"Ye've filled the room with the sweet smell of hot scones! It'll not do, lassie! I've trouble enough with this!" John slapped his portly stomach. "I've a feeling you've got something on your mind, lass."

"Uncle, you know how I have often come down and helped out filing receipts, checking orders for sails and ropes for the next ships or repairs …?"

"Yes, lass."

"Why couldn't I be *making* the orders for Anderson's and Co, Fraser & Tinne, Lloyd's, carpenters Brain and Bishop?"

"What are you saying, Phem?"

"Times are changing. I want to be an independent woman, not necessarily under my husband's permissions. I knew nothing about shipping till I got dropped in, you could say, the deep end." We both laughed. "I do not know whether you heard, but last week I went and spoke to Maggie's class about Father's history. I spent a few evenings before he left going over stories from the past. It made me want to know more about the business."

Uncle John looked at me intently as I spoke.

"For as long as I can remember, Father's been talking ships, scheming a new route, securing new suppliers: potatoes from Canterbury, coal from Greymouth or Newcastle, fruit from Fiji, Guano from the islands. I know there are two things he loves most: great design and good craftsmen!"

"He also loves to give exceptional quality and get quality in return, at a fair price, but you forgot one thing."

"What's that?"

"Murdoch is the oldest son." John had a twinkle in his eye.

"I am not asking to take over Murdoch's role with the shipping … I guess what I'm saying is, I know him! Of course, normally a son would be trained up to carry on the business side! But why not *me*!"

Uncle John studied me with great intent. "Lassie, perhaps it is time we brought you up to speed with your family history, you have a flair for business that your Father has spoken of. I had not thought of it before but what if *he* says no?"

"Then what have I lost? I do not see why the boys should have all the reponsibility."

"He does need the help and he would rather be out on the seas than stuck in the office. You would be freeing him up to do what is his true passion – taming the deep!"

We both roared with laughter.

"Uncle, before we launch into history, how do you think Father is? I am quite worried about him! Before he left, I have not seen him so troubled."

Uncle John looked directly at me without blinking. "Don't ye worry your head none, your pappy's the toughest, smartest captain that e're lived!!" He picked up his letter opener and flicked it about nervously as if avoiding something.

"I know you always say that. It is just … I … I … What if it is something quite terrible? He could be terminally sick and does not want us to know. He has looked pale lately. I wish he would send word; it is the hardest thing about waiting at home, not knowing!"

"I bet you'll look up any day now and that tubby wee boat'll be cumin' 'n docks."

I put my head down, wanting so to tell him about the letter. *But what if Father is keeping it a secret from Uncle as well?*

"Now, now, don't you go getting upset. He has had a lot to deal with, lassie, with the *Presto* and ol' *Frankie*. Sit ye self down. I was looking over our old books last week – took a few hours

– just records from the past few years. I guess you could call it 'taking stock', 'cause with the repairs we have made on ol' *Frankie*, well, it is not going well, and it needs a sharp mind to account for it all. I have my own things to deal with too. Why don't you make some tea, and I will tidy my desk so we can go over a few things? I can give you about two hours this morning."

"Would you!? Oh, that would be wonderful!"

Chapter 12

Lessons in the Office

Father's desk was perfectly arranged and tidied away, but Uncle's was more like a biological organ, not a heart but perhaps a liver, full of a hundred things that needed sorting or seeing to.

I walked past Father's office and opened the door, saw his old leather chair and a portrait of Mother on the wall. I forgot how pretty she was – everyone said I looked like her.

Aunt Sarah had left the kettle quietly heating on the range, and I even found butter in the cooler. The teacups I recognised from the glass cabinet that stood at Uncle Johns house, in his sitting room. We were never allowed in there when we were little, except at Christmas time for shortbread and sweet mince pies. While the family gathered, we would sing songs with Sarah on the piano.

"Good morning, Phee. Lovely to see you. How are all the children?" Aunt Sarah also kept some of the accounts for Father.

"Aunt Sarah, the children are fine, although Hannah always finds it hard each time Father sets sail. She caught Murdoch's influenza two weeks back and cried for Mother. I do my best to distract her. You know what it is like? Maggie and I are making a mat, which Mother had half-finished, for her bedroom floor. It will make it warmer on the floor by her bed at least.

"That sounds lovely. What is it made of?"

"We've made it from strips of material cut up from hand-me-down clothes Hannah has grown out of. Actually, our hooks are almost worn out." We both laughed. "Would you like a scone? Sorry I have no cream."

"Oh, these are lovely, Phee, just the way I like them, slightly crunchy and soft inside. This jam is good!"

"We made it from the apricots on our tree last January. How are you going?"

"I am good, but there seems to be more and more government restrictions in shipping. It was so much simpler before the unions started getting on their high horses."

"Will I see you at the next Temperance meeting?"

"Yes, of course! Well, I must get back. Uncle John's giving me an interesting history lesson of the last decade at the yard."

"That will certainly leave your brain taxed. Good luck!"

I could hear chopping and grinding coming from the big shed as I went down the hall. I caught a glimpse of her hull through the double doors as I passed by. "Oh sorry!" I reeled.

Duncan had come through the doorway at that exact same instant.

"Sorry, Miss, I nearly knocked over your scones. How are you? How is the Captain?"

He had the most vibrant red hair under his cloth hat. *I must keep my head.*

"Duncan, how lovely to see you! Sorry I did not stop to talk earlier. It has been a little while. Father is away at present; I am expecting him any day now! I had forgotten you worked here!"

"Perhaps you have missed me a few times as I am often working on a repair in the port?"

I wanted to say I had 'missed you', the fact is I never really noticed him at all before my dream. Now my own heart was about to betray my true feelings.

"That must be what it is. Timing! What are you working on?"

"It is a little boat they were going to christen *Tonga*."

"It is always a hive of activity and hard to believe it's all tidied up sometimes for official launching celebrations."

I had lost track of time, and my uncle's tea was now almost cold. "I am sorry, I must go. I will be about a little more, perhaps I will see you another day!"

"I would like that, Miss."

I was still trembling slightly when I placed Uncle's tea on his somewhat tidier desk, and it slopped slightly into the saucer. I placed the china plate down with a scone layered in butter and jam.

"Are you alright lass, ye look like you have just seen a ghost!"

"I got a fright running into Duncan."

"Ah, fine family. These are great. Did ye make 'em ye self?"

"I have been doing projects with Hannah to take her mind off Father *and* Barbara being absent."

"I love the jam! Now I know you have a real desire to show the Captain your stubborn passion. I am all for women taking on new roles. You have a great head on your shoulders, lass. I have also seen you carry great passion for shipping, both the business and with people. But … you will have to prove it to me. It is a man's world down here, lass, you will have to be tough."

I was more determined than ever to show Uncle I was not wasting his time.

"Let us bring ye up to speed – hoist a few sails as it were, and steer a fresh course. Or maybe for you as a woman it will be like starting with a half-finished canvas. We will add some splashes of colour, a few joys and sorrows, losses, and victories. Why I've no doubt you have a few colours you could add of your own!"

I could see where Uncle's mind was going. Perhaps he was weighing up what Father might say, and was he betraying Murdoch?

"Okay, okay then. It is already August 93, so let's take our paintbrushes and go back to say, 1867. I heard from a few folks that you did your father proud at the school a few weeks back!"

"Thank you, Uncle, but I'm even more nervous now because I've been asked by Mrs Laird to go and speak to the class again."

"Well, let us get on then —I'm guessing more than twenty ships built … bought, and easily double that again with major repairs and untold trips to sea. You might have to come back for more lessons. It is all recorded here somewhere in my little brown book.

"Oh, here it is!"

Uncle John held up a brown book with leather binding and a tiny gold trim. He rose to his feet and announced, "Come with me!"

As we walked along the hall out to the yard, he said, "Your Father seems tireless; he keeps inspiring me. Long before we have a new boat ready to launch, he has plans drawn up and the timber already seasoning in the yard for another. Is it not the prettiest sight to watch a new boat come to life, each day a new rib, plank … it is the finishing that takes time. But one year, in 1875, we built four ships. The *Roderick Dhu* alone was a beauty, one of three sister ships, all big, three-masted schooners over 300 ton loaded."

We stood looking at the skeleton of a small ship up on the slipway, already sitting on two long kauri rails for her to have her chocks removed and slide into the ocean.

"What do you see?"

"I have always thought ships look like the rib cage of a chicken, upside down. A backbone, ribs extending up and then a skin fitted to the outside."

"Well, I'll be, lass! Never have I heard it explained so simply! Of course, you are precisely right. Once we have the chicken carcass up and the skin on, we tie all the timbers together to form the decks. Then the masts are lifted into place and the real work begins with finishing the ship off – decks, cabins, hatches, rudder and of course all the rigging. You will need to know each piece because there are always repairs to do and orders to be made. As soon as you start to learn these parts, it will come together quickly because you have sailed with your father many times and you will remember him talking about parts of a ship your whole life. Come, let us go back to the office."

Father had bought John out of the partnership many years ago, but he still worked for him. They were a good team. Father was all the practical side of the business, but the office was where Uncle John's skills kicked in, as a Master ships agent.

"I see Uncle John … catch the scent of another buyer and track them down like a bloodhound."

"Well, it is the Captain who dreams the design into life, leaving no detail out for the build. He cannot help his Scottish roots in snapping up a bargain when a ship comes to grief and can be rebuilt."

"I watched the progress with the repairs to the *Waireka* after weeks of work re-floating her off the rocks at Kawau island. The Northern steamship company employed McQuarrie and McCallum to refit her."

"Yes, lass, we thought it was never going to re-float. I think after a month they would not let it beat them!"

"It feels to me like pulling knitting to pieces. When I find a mistake and have to pull it apart again. It must be heartbreaking for you, launching a glorious new ship only to then turn around and fix her up again when she is half broken."

"I must admit it does smart seeing a ship come to grief, but so many are lost on these rocky coasts. Many of our ships only last five years. But who better to do the repair than its original craftsman?

"Did you ever read the article about the *Waireka*? I have a book I have called *Glory* of all the old reviews I have saved from the newspapers." Uncle flipped through a book full of newspaper clippings. "Here it is."

"*Waireka*, there'd never been a finer ship to come into the Auckland harbour. The article says …

> *The Waireka is now on her maiden trip. She was built by Mr. Hector McQuarrie, of Auckland, to the order of her commander, Captain G. Johnson. Her hull is shapely and her masts have a slight rake, which certainly does not detract from her appearance. The vessel is named after the title given to the first engagement between the rebel Maoris and the militia and volunteers at Taranaki.*
>
> *Captain Webster, who commanded No. 9 company of volunteers at that engagement, is a*

passenger by the Waireka. During the run across, the Waireka has not only proved herself as a very fast vessel, having come from land to land in seven days, but also demonstrated she is an excellent sea boat."

Chapter 13

Slavery & Black Birding

"You know, lass, a couple of years back Captain Urquhart went before the judge in desperate times and owed us more than £500. The judge asked Hector what he would like to do as the principal debt was owed to him? Your father said 'As the Captain has come on hard times and he is a fellow Highlander, I would like the debt withdrawn'."

"Uncle, I had no idea! We could do with the money now, that must be the equivalent to the profit of one whole build?"

"Yes, lassie, you certainly have a flair for business and a good head. Your sister is a brilliant mathematician – looks like you both have your own gifts. I wonder if it had been you what your decision would have been?"

"I am not sure, but I have noticed with Father, sometimes in business the best decisions are not always the wisest financial ones. Father would say 'The Lord is no man's debtor, He provides everything."

"Anyway, a few months later Captain Urquhart's debt of £500 we wrote off.

"The *Scotia* fund, Uncle?"

"Yes The *Scotia* fund, and I think a young man will soon discover you just like gold."

I could feel my cheeks flush with delight. I could not hide my desire to have the attention of a delicious young man. I tried not to think of Duncan being only yards away. It would be good to spend more time here and not only to dive into Father's business! Father oversaw all the hiring of the men and Uncle left the heavy work to him.

"Hector has such a passion for great design, that is why the Northern Steamship Company commissioned us to build the first Tug Steamer. The *Awhina* is 300 horsepower driven from two engines."

"That is a lot, is it not, Uncle?"

"That's a whole paddock of horses, Phee! The *Rowena* is barely half that but let us not get ahead of ourselves."

The Awhina

"I think Mother was pregnant then with Hannah at that time. Father would often talk ship design with her. She was very patient, listening intently, and I think in some ways it helped him to speak it out."

John rubbed his forehead. "Is it that long? Time has flown

by! Yes, I have had many of those conversations too. A new faster design, flatter bottomed hull that can carry a bigger payload and still get into the shallow coastal beaches. Sleeker for speed, bigger hatches to load more easily, larger ballast tanks to offset a load.

"Lass, I have had a few blows too! We had a build last year and at the last minute the customer wanted to raise the poop deck a foot. We were already behind starting the next build."

"You are right, Uncle. He sees it all as a challenge to conquer but he can be stubborn alright. I have seen him push the boundaries, squeeze in another quick job, get a little more speed, help another desperate captain in hard times. He is passionate but with a huge heart."

"*MacGregor* for the Northern Steam Ship Company, named of course after John McGregor, the director. She was the first decent size steamer we had built. She was 282 tons."

"I have no problem telling folk that my father built this beauty."

"The Captain was quietly proud of her alright! We got the decorators in and no expense was spared."

"Father proudly took us as a family down one Saturday and gave us a guided tour of every last detail before her sea trial. I still remember walking into the lady's lounge. That sweet scent of new fabric and fresh linseed oil on the timber; private seating with plush light-blue seats and décor to match. A separate lady's bathroom and powder room with big mirrors and hot running water."

"Phee, these chairs we are sitting on were covered with the remaining fabric!" Uncle rubbed his hands on the fabric with pride. "She was meant to do 8 to 10 knots maximum, but even in her trials she did 12 and 13. We were chewing through the coal that day!”

“Now we come back to *Awhina* built for the local Waitemata. She was born out of the need to rescue ships in distress or wrecks run aground. We had great support from the local shipping community because huge ships were coming in under sail but in a storm, they could not get to the wharf. There is only so much can be done with a few men pulling in rowboats. As ships came alongside, they would hit the wharf and repairs were constantly being made. She was also called upon to do all sorts of manoeuvres.

“One such case was a man who urgently needed to be rescued from Great Barrier Island. He had an emergency operation after being brought back to Auckland.

“She has pulled many ships off rocks and sandy beaches, including Waireka at Kawau. She has a shallow hull so she can get in close to shore.

“*Bannockburn* in late 84 wrecked off Rockhampton. She was a total wreck and, of course, we suffered a huge loss due to being under-insured. Our 16th share each meant we had not taken a profit on the build.”

“What did the insurance cover?”

“Barely the shipment of timber.”

“She was like one of three sisters, *Meg Merrilee’s*, *Clansman* and *Bannockburn* built in 1879. Those were good days: we were turning those ships out like a sausage machine,” he said, laughing.

“Uncle, wasn’t the *Meg Merrilee’s* a slave-trading ship?”

“We do not like to call it slave-trading. Slave-trading was abolished before you were born, lass, but I think what you mean is ‘Blackbirding!’, which has come to an end thankfully.”

“Oh, I recently read *The History of Shipping,* about a ship called the *Daphne* caught 'Blackbirding' around 1867. She was boarded, and the hold full of Islanders was kidnapped and lured to Queensland for the sugar industry. Apparently, tens of thousands have been enslaved there, forced at gunpoint, kidnapped or bribed through local chiefs to board ships and in many cases, sold."

Meg Merrilee's, one of three sister ships

"I think that is strong language, but I cut out an article a few years back about a ship called the *Wild Duck*. It was sailing around Santos Island in the Hebrides, along with another ship the *Lulu*, blackbirding. When their small party went ashore, 150 natives came out shouting and blowing conch shells. Even though one crewman had lived there for a time, they were all murdered, and the ship only just escaped the canoes full of islanders about to board her and take her over."

"You do have an article from June 10th, 1870 about the *LuLu* caught bringing twenty-seven South Sea Islanders right into our port in Auckland? They were brought in to work in the flax fields and mill at Waitakere. It says their own chiefs were lured with gifts, and they were contracted to stay for three years. It says, the Auckland papers are unanimous in condemning this importation, thinking, as we do, that it is only slavery clumsily disguised, similar to that which has caused such scandal in Fiji, Queensland and other places. A Fiji paper reported the unfortunate Melanesians are kidnapped and actually sold like merchandise.

"Is that true, Euphemia? I have heard the South Sea Islanders are paid about £6 a year …

"… and can they go home at any time?"

"Most sign a contract for forty years."

"How is it any different to slavery? They are paid what a man here would make in a matter of weeks. Its hard labour and for forty years away from their home, village, culture, poor living conditions. Is that not like slavery?"

"That is a blunt assessment of the situation. You have the right tack to chase down our debtors and negotiate with you!"

"But it is true. Did Father ever use his ships to Blackbird?"

"No, of course not! It is a terrible thing. There are too many sad stories of people being separated from their loved ones, children, wives, in the hope they would get fair work and conditions. When you build a ship, you cannot tell someone what it can be used for. Perhaps it was fortuitous that the Meg was shipwrecked. But do not forget, she was a beauty."

"Uncle, there is one about her here: The *Meg Merilee's* was one of the prettiest ships ever to grace the Waitemata Harbour. She beat all the speed records from Auckland to Melbourne."

"Listen to this one! The *Clansman* was launched on a holiday, and folks came from everywhere to watch. They had buntings flying on the houses along the waterfront and over the five ships in the harbour."

"If I remember rightly, there was a reverend on board who recalled a conversation with your father saying. 'when are you going to bring one of your steamers down here to Waitara?' Hector said, 'Don't you already have one?'"

"'No!' said the reverend. Your father said, 'What about the *Hauraki*?' To which the whole ship full of dignitaries erupted in laughter. She was just a little steamboat running up the rivers."

"I do not remember the *Hauraki*? But how do you fund the build of such big ships?"

"If it is a ship being built for a customer, they pay us progress payments – when the stem is laid, the ribs are finished, the decks are fitted etc. Otherwise, we offer up Shares, and we cover the cost. The *Scotia* fund has helped to have ships fully paid for."

"Scotia? Oh, yes, I am sure it has helped many times. Do you mean there were plenty of investors applying for shares?"

"Aye, lass. Once word got out that we were building the fastest, reliable ships, we had many enquiries for shares. We offered shares to investors from the moment we lay the main stem. It generally takes us six months to build one and send her gliding into the water and the next day start another.

"What about seasoned timber?"

"The Captain delivers timber from mills all over Auckland, so he sources the best heart kauri and stacks it to dry. We have a year's supply at any one time.

"Sometimes before the ships are finished, they can be fully funded, but of course, sometimes we carry the remainder if the shares are not taken up. This way, we also earn a return for the business. It is like they pay rent."

"That is if it does not get shipwrecked," I said, smiling.

"Yes, I know your father has huge respect for some Captains who do not take risks and who are honest and true. He despises those who take short cuts and have little regard for the ship's owner."

"Especially after the *Flying Cloud* incident."

Uncle put his head down and said, "Let us move on!

"The *Curlew*. I can see by your face, lassie; your father had a soft spot for her."

"I think he put so much into the *Curlew*. The nearest bird I have seen was an owl calling at night "Moorpork! Moorpork!" but Father took me on a trip way up the coast of Australia to Townsville. I kept waking at night to a blood-curdling scream. These long-legged birds wander about at night calling to one another. They sound like a woman being murdered. But when they soar, they have a huge wingspan."

"Do you think, lass, that is what he had in mind?"

"I do not know but I think it is Scott's famous lines that make more sense. 'Sharp as the shriek of the curlew from Craig to Craig the signal flew'."

"That could be it. She has been darting all over the north into little settlements delivering goods and picking up flax."

Uncle rocked back in his chair "I just remember watching little Maggie standing on that high platform. It was the Christmas break of 86. She was about eleven and looked like an angel in her white dress. She shouted out 'I Christen you Curlew' at the top of her voice!"

Uncle John started to laugh, which looked funny as his portly tummy wiggled.

"She smashed that bottle with such determination it

exploded into tiny pieces on the front bow, splashing bystanders four feet away. I think Hector must have explained, 'A ship'll be cursed if the champagne'll not bath her bow, so give it a good hard swing!'" He was now laughing so hard, he had to wipe away the tears from his face. "I loved her triumphant face as the ship gently slid down into the waves … still gives me goosebumps."

"I must remind Maggie about her launching the *Curlew* when I get home."

"Your father took the opportunity to Captain *Curlew* between builds in August 87. Weren't you about ten years old around 1880, when he asked *you* if you'd like to christen the *Cutty Sark*. She was only a wee boat of 50 ton but you were shy and decided at the last minute you couldn't do it."

"I was nervous of the glass breaking over the gathered crowd."

"Well, it might be a good opportunity to stop there and resume our training in a few days."

"Really, Uncle?. I cannot thank you enough for your time. It will be perfect timing as I put a big roast of lamb in the range to cook slowly. I will get home and do the vegetables for dinner. I will try and bring you some shortbread next time I come."

"You have done well, lass. Give your family my love!"

I leaned over and gave him a kiss before I headed out. As I quietly closed the door behind me, I felt charged with courage and excitement, wondering what Father's response would be to my proposal.

Chapter 14

Strong Values

Eileen came over early the next morning. She had guests coming Saturday night for dinner and wanted to catch up on a few things she'd left undone the day before. As I went looking for her, I passed Mary's old room, and my mind wandered off as I remembered her, just younger than Maggie was now at fourteen. It would be nearly five years in October. She'd been so beautiful; none of us had had the courage to clear out her room, because it made it so final.

Dong! Dong!

"Oh, goodness!" I gasped in fright as the clock next to me suddenly chimed ten. Bessy came out from hiding to find me, as Eileen called from the drawing-room:

"Are you okay, lass?"

As I came round the corner, there was Eileen on her knees with the hearth shovel clearing the ash from the firebox.

"There you are! Goodness me, I was not expecting the clock to ring out right beside me as I was daydreaming about Mary. I just came to ask if you would like tea? I have a surprise today for you this time! I know you've been too busy to bake this week.

"Well, you know how I love surprises; I will be there in a minute. Let me just finish clearing the ash from the hearth and I'll be right out."

I quickly poured the tea and got out the shortbread I had tried to re-create for Eileen. I'd remembered a tip passed on from my great grandmother …whip the butter and sugar furiously, add a tiny bit of icing sugar and they would come out light, fluffy and white. Eileen swung around the corner with her apron on. She had a motherly face with fine wispy hair and a little bonnet fastened to her head. When she grinned, her whole face lit up.

"How exciting! Aww! I do love surprises. Well I'll be! Shortbread. How on earth did you get them so white, lass?"

"It is Granny's recipe!"

She took a bite, and her eyes became as big as saucers. "Wait till the ladies at embroidery hear about this, it is sooo light!"

I was feeling so thrilled; each new thing I learned seemed like a victory.

"Have you received a letter from Barbara yet?"

"No, not yet. A telegram came in the third week saying they had made it safely to Melbourne on the 24th and off-loaded the timber successfully, but it would be nice to have a few more details." I dare not tell her of the sealed letter for the Captain.

"I hope Barbara's letter comes soon. All I know is they were headed to New South Wales to pick up coal which I had seen on the cargo documents in the office."

"The Captain has been away now since late May. Seven weeks already. I hope he has had a good run. Naturally, you can't help worrying."

"I woke in the early hours of the morning worrying last night, about the grief Father has suffered. First Margaret and Mary – his wife and daughter in Mull. Then Murdoch before I was born, at six months. Annie too, at only a year old. She was my favourite – nursing her was never a chore, even when she threw up once on my favourite blue dress. Then Mother and our Mary! So much sadness, we hardly have room on the mantlepiece for them all."

"I had forgotten about the Captain's first family."

"Yes, Father was thirty-four when he came to New Zealand searching for a better life. Grief-stricken after losing his son, Murdoch, then his wife, Margaret, and finally his daughter, Mary, he boarded a ship in Liverpool and worked his passage as a ship's carpenter. Knowing that Sir George Gray had helped a large Scottish Highland community take up land in New Zealand, and hearing stories on the wind of a gold rush in Victoria, he had hope of a new life here."

"If I remember, everyone was starving in Scotland and Ireland with the potato blight of 1845. What a dreadful thing, and not a nice thing to think about in the middle of the night!"

"Eileen, don't you hate waking in the middle of the night and just lying there worrying. Thoughts seem insurmountable, like problems with no solution, then in the morning, you wonder why you were so concerned!"

We laughed together.

"I also woke the other night worrying about what I would make for the luncheon for the new Reverend?"

"Phee, how did it go?"

"It was quite exciting. We all welcomed him and his family to Parnell Rise. Do you know, I could not decide which dress to wear. I tried two completely different outfits. I even sneaked in and tried Maggie's white dress! I could not even get the buttons done up on it!"

"Oh, to be slim again like Maggie." Eileen laughed. "So, what *did* you wear?"

"Of course, my favourite blue taffeta."

"I haven't seen that for a while. Does it still fit you?"

"It was a little tight around the bust." We both laughed. "Mr Knox officiated. He stood and welcomed the Kelly family to our church." Bess came from her warm spot in the sun and sniffed about looking for a few crumbs. I threw her a piece of bread I had drying above the range.

"Do continue!" Eileen patted her and scratched behind her ears.

"John and Elizabeth Knox have been looking to raise funds."

"Good girl, Bessie! Phee, I have heard Reverend Kelly has plans for the new church!"

"Yes, they have some great plans. Did you know that Reverend Kelly was originally from Lanarkshire in the Highlands?"

"Yes, but he is more recently from Waimate in Oamaru, I think?"

"He looks slightly serious, don't you think? And balding, but a real sparkle through his round spectacles."

"Master Kelly looked dashing in his waistcoat and his wild red hair swished back on Sunday. I saw you looking at him."

"He has the bluest eyes. I caught Ernest looking at me across the room and, for a second, he smiled at me. I felt my face flush. It is like Duncan, this boy I went to school with. He was this tubby little lad with fat cheeks. I saw him at Father's old yard, and I was so nervous I could not speak! He has grown into a handsome, muscular man."

"Oh, Phemie! How old is he?"

"Well I'm not sure, but I think he must be about twenty-one."

"You need to be looking for a more mature man with

means!"

"Don't you mean an older man, because I'm past marrying age at twenty-three? I will only meet a man whose wife has died and needs a mother to look after the children."

Eileen stared at me shocked and utterly taken aback.

"Euphemia, that was very spirited! No, not at all! I just mean someone who has been waiting to come along and sweep you off your feet."

"I'm sorry, Eileen, I should not have said that. It's just that there's huge pressure to marry when you get to twenty-one and I am not sure I am one of those women with traditional values."

"I know Reverend Kelly has strong traditional values. He said he believes that a women's place is in the home and all this talk of women working in men's jobs is wicked. He said 'I aim at making the Bible a book for the times, and at bringing young men under Christian influence'."

"Father would support him wholeheartedly as far as encouraging sobriety with young men, both because he's a fellow highlander and employing so many young men in the yards and at sea. He'd probably say more young men could do with a little good Christian influence."

"And it's also good for the boys with the Captain away so much. The twins are starting high school next year. Perhaps the Captain hopes to send them to study for business."

"This is exactly what I mean. Why shouldn't I be trained to take over? Why does it have to be Murdoch, the oldest? There was a time I had hoped I could study commerce; perhaps go to Cambridge in Britain. I had asked Father and at the time he was in full support. He preferred I went to study in Melbourne so he could see me every few months. Now with Mother's passing and Barbara sick, money's tight. He needs me to manage the house."

"You are right. The Captain would say exactly that, and he has liberal support for you girls. But do not forget your place in society, Phem!"

My ears were burning now, I could feel rage welling up. I was about to burst! Bess suddenly barked and ran to the front door. At the same moment, there was a shout and knock on the door.

"Only me … Aunty Christine."

"We are in the kitchen," I shouted.

She took off her coat and came through to the kitchen.

"Looks like I came at the right time! I just thought I would call in on my way home and drop off a huge fish I was given at the port. She placed the paper packet on the bench and wrapped her arms around me tightly.

"Are you alright? You seem stiff. Did I come at a bad time?"

I didn't know why my reaction was so strong "No, it is fine. Will you stay, Aunt? You know Mrs Davis? I will top up the teapot! How are you?"

"Oh, lovely to see you, Mrs Davis. You are such a dear helping my niece. I would love to stay but I only called for a minute to see how you are going?" She fixed her eyes on mine and said, "I think I already know," with a little giggle. "Now what are you two discussing? It looks serious. Go on, pour me a cup."

"I was rather rude to Eileen a few minutes ago as we discussed traditional values and how a woman should behave in society."

"Well, there's an interesting thing, Phem. Do you remember Kate Sheppard a year past? She came speaking about suffrage women with the Women's League?"

"Yes, she's my heroine. I added my signature to petitions that thousands of women all over New Zealand have presented to parliament three years running."

"Well, I was in Queen Street a few hours ago. She had set up a soapbox in the square, challenging women to use their influence to vote in the upcoming elections."

Queen Street, Auckland

"How exciting, Aunt. This is why we are attending the Temperance meetings. You should come, Eileen!"

"I do not think so, lass!"

"Ladies, there was a real buzz in the air. Kate's reminding women they have the right to own land already, and to be ready to vote, and even one day, women doing men's jobs. She has stirred up a hornet's nest since last year. A huge crowd of women were standing listening and applauding. They talked of prohibition and men being at home for their families. You should have seen the disgruntled looks on some of the men's faces standing listening or walking by. I think they might be scared we will all run off and become doctors and lawyers or something."

"Or vote for total prohibition!" I said.

Eileen had sat holding her hands tightly, fidgeting with a ring on one finger.

"Perhaps shipbuilders!" Aunt Christine and I laughed. "Do you really think the male majority government will consider equal rights for women?"

Eileen, nervously wiping her hands on her apron, looked quite uncomfortable. She said, "We don't want to stir things up too much, do we, ladies? Remember your place."

"On the contraire, Eileen. I think it's high time there was some stirring going on! I wonder what would happen if we refused to have food on the table for one week, wash men's clothes, or care for the children. I might even try that with the boys tonight."

"Now, Phem, you will never hook a man with that attitude."

"You must admit, Mrs Davis, it would be fun to try."

Eileen rose to her feet. "Now I do think it's all got out of hand, ladies. You know, Christine, a woman's place is in the home as a mother looking after the children, keeping the home ready for her husband. I hate to think what could happen if suddenly mothers started running off to employment instead of being at home. What about the children!?"

"Well I think it's about time we stood up for ourselves and had more women in men's jobs! I'm going to be one of the first women in the world to get an equal vote in this election. I cannot wait!"

"Ladies, I must get on. Please excuse me." Christine gathered up her bag, thanked Mrs Davis, kissed me on the cheek and was gone.

Chapter 15

Shipping History 2

I had gripped the balcony rail at sunrise that morning and carefully held Grandfather McLeod's old monocular to one eye. My heart raced as I spotted white sails, but it was only a two-mast, fore and aft boat that looked a lot like *Onward*. Murdoch had joined me a few times in the last few days looking out to sea.

"Murdoch, I know it will not help to worry but the last time I went with Father to sea for a load of coal we had a frightful passage. The wind came up as we headed out into deep waters and the boat was tossed terribly. In the end, they had to drop the mainsail in case we broke a mast. It makes me feel small and frail when at the mercy of the elements."

"I love it, Phem – the rougher the better. I have never felt unsafe with Father. No matter how strong the wind, rain or storms, Father seems fearless. He stands locked in a contest again the wind. It is a fearsome sight. His whiskers held tight under the strap of his oilskin hat, his ruddy cheeks glow as he stands fast at the helm, braced against the winds and spray.

"Oh, you men! Although, I do remember once I fought my way out of the cabin in ferocious seas and through the spray. I saw the Captain lashed to the helm, waves breaking over the bow and him singing an old hymn at the top of his voice." We both roared with laughter.

"That is him alright – it is in his blood. Still, he has a fearful respect for the sea."

"Call it instinct or something, I feel that something is wrong all the same. Just a glimpse of familiar white wings flying on old *Frankie* would make my day."

"It's a strain to see any sails today through the smog and mist. And the cold has a real bite. On clear days you can see straight through the cut, right out past Waiheke and Jackson's point to Great Barrier Island."

"You are right, Murdoch. Not today! I seem to catch sight of every old barque coming into the harbour as I go about the house doing chores."

The twins burst in. "What can you see?"

"Oh, of course, we are looking for *Frankie*. Here, take a look."

The twins argued over who had a longer go.

"Look, there's a man up that mast, and she's flying the Union Jack. It is not hard to tell one boat from another!"

Ken was more interested in where the steamers were headed.

"I think that one is off to Kawau Island."

"Here, give Dug a turn. You have to check how low they are in the water. Old *Frankie's* usually full to the gunnels with sawn timber, but she'll be carrying over 200 ton of coal from Newcastle this time."

"Father says 'the old barque's not fast but what she lacks in speed she makes up in the carrying'."

"She might be an old working hulk, but Father sails her like his princess."

"Somehow, I am wishing she will come into view around the heads doing any speed at all."

The smell of coal wafting up from the harbour accompanies the sound of low thuds of the big steam engines.

"So many steamers these days, I miss the old sailing ships with their angel wings fluttering like linen sheets on the line."

"When the northerly's up, Maggie, you can hear shouts from the sailors trimming the sails as they head out on another adventure at sea."

The children headed away to school and I went with them halfway, leaving Murdoch at home today. I bought a copy of the *Auckland Star* again on the way home to check any articles about the *Frank Guy* and Kate Sheppard and the suffragettes.

I came back in and there was a telegram reply from Barbara sitting on the table.

Dear Euphemia

Telegram received gladly. Happy all is well. Repairs to Rudder. Coal loaded. Heading out. Hope for good run to Auckland. Fondly Barbara.

It seemed Father and his indomitable spirit had the consignment organised with old *Frankie*. I packed my little bag and went off to Uncle John's office.

I carried the little parcel of shortbread in one hand looking about the yard for Duncan as I passed through. "Good morning, Uncle. I have been looking forward to coming and catching up on more of our history.

"I brought shortbread this time; I know they are your favourite."

"You really do know a man's heart, don't you, lass. So where did we get to? Ah! here it is. I saved it with a bookmark. The *Gailoch*!"

"You even kept this article too. It says in the *Wellington Times*

'It was a huge success. The hull appears to be seamless as to its repair. You could not tell where it had been joined."

"This is truly where your father excels! Only a brave man with courage would go for three months to another city like Wellington, cut a sailing ship in half, lengthen it, change the cabins to fit ballast tanks, then fit a steam engine; making room for the water tanks. The ballast tanks alone would frighten any shipwright, let alone fitting an engine, propellers, boiler and heat proofing. He had to work with foreign engineers, fitters, carpenters and decorators too. It was a good thing he insisted on taking some of our crew."

"Are these contracts lucrative? I do not know how Father can be in all places at once, one-minute sailing off to New South Wales, then overseeing a build in Thames or Auckland, then undertaking repairs elsewhere! No wonder he is never home!"

"It has not been all plain sailing. We must take work sometimes where we can. Times are tough right now. Contracting and building ships for big companies can cut our prices to the bone. With so many shipbuilders up here in the North, competition's fierce. We quoted and won a job the other day stripping and re-metaling a ship, with six days to do it. There was seven quotes and only £60 difference. The unions have not made it easy either. The ship owners were getting harassed by the unions, so we formed our own Association of ship owners. It has given us the power to push back, and in the last few years, they are almost non-existent. Our men are happy with ten shillings a day and we have been fortunate to have such wonderful workmen."

"The *Mariner*? Was that one of ours?"

"No, lass but I cut it out 'cause what a passage! Well, I can laugh now but at the time the Captain came through that door more than a little bit humbled."

"Why?"

"He had just returned from the Philippines on the *Mariner* from Manilla and was shattered! Thirty-one days of hell, squalls, thunder, lightning, torrents of rain and they almost lost her to the sea. The ship was laying over till the lee rail was under water! How he saved the ship's cargo I will never know?"

"What was it carrying?"

"A full load of fruit on board. I can hardly fathom how it was still alright and able to be sold."

"Fresh fruit from the tropics. I love it when Father brings coconuts and mangos back from Fiji."

Just then there was a knock on the door and a well-dressed gentleman entered.

"Good morning, John. Shall I come back another time when it is convenient?"

"No, this is my niece. We are just going over a few things. Euphemia, meet Mr Collins."

"Lovely to meet you, sir. Can I make you a cup of tea?"

"That would be lovely, thank you."

"Splendid, lass! I think we need a break. Pity there are no mangoes!"

I took the door to the big shed. It had a blacksmith shop in one corner. My heart pounded as I looked around again for Duncan, who should have been at the wharf doing repairs.

"Morning, lassie. Captain's away!"

"Morning, Monk!" He was a tubby, little man in a blackened leather apron; bald except for a little hair around the base of his head, making him look like a monk. I was poised and on guard, trying my best to be invisible. It was mostly a cheery environment as shipwrights and carpenters sometimes broke out in a Scottish Highland song.

"Morning, Bash'in! What have you got on the slip?"

"Euphemia, my dear! It is a tiny little ship, only eleven ton; it will soon have its chocks removed and the masts fitted alongside the wharf.

"Phee, how are we so lucky to have ye grace us today?"

"I am here doing some work for Uncle John and thought I would bring him some shortbread."

"Next time, lass, throw a few more in the range; we'll not say no!"

"Alright, I will."

Bash'in swung the huge hammer and bashed in the wooden nails that held the planking on the ship, although more recently copper nails were being used. It was a tedious job for a few men shaping wooden nails and drying them. Copper nails from Fraser & Tinne were more expensive but did speed up the process. They were imported from England, but the men hate them as they were soft and could bend if there was a hard knot in the timber.

"Bash'in, is Duncan around today?"

"Yes, he is down at the Queen Street wharf today doing repairs. Do you want me to get a lad to fetch him?"

"Oh no, I was just curious. Thanks for your help."

I made the tea and left it a few minutes to draw then took it back in. "There's your tea and a few of your favourite biscuits made with Gran's recipe."

"That was a customer securing a load of water pumps to go to Thames. They use them for flooding in the mining tunnels. Do you know they say there is a greater population of people living in Thames than the whole of Auckland City? I find that hard to believe."

"Well, Uncle, I heard that is quite true."

"Not that I am ungrateful, lass; it has carried us through, shipping plenty of goods and passengers."

"I have not been there yet. Maggie went with Father on a trip to check on a ship's progress. Nicolai told me it is no place for a woman."

Uncle threw his head back and laughed. "The only ones who need be afraid are the men of Thames, of you. You go next time the Captain goes to the shipyard there. The gold in Thames was the only thing that saved us from Mr Quartier and the *Flying Cloud* debacle."

"I spoke to Maggie's class about the miracle of the *Flying Cloud*. Father helped go over the details of the story."

"That was a most terrible time, Phem. Many thought it was our fault! Well, we must press on – this shortbread is superb, light and crisp. Now where were we … oh yes … the *Gael*.

You might remember a trip the Captain took up to Fiji, to buy the *Gael*. He bought it on tender for £505. Honestly, I thought he had paid too much. It got wrecked on the rocks on an island called Ovalau, in Fiji, but he managed to get her off and repaired. We had built that ship from new and we knew she had been all re-coppered. We ran her for a bit then sold her to Captain McCleod.

"It says here 'Sadly, she was wrecked in '89'."

"Yes, that was sad. But what was truly sad was, in '87 we started fighting this bankruptcy business."

"Uncle John, Barbara and I have watched Father some days walk out like a shadow, like someone had drained the life right out of him. Even when he was home, he was a vapour of himself. He went off to those court hearings like a dead man."

"It was a hard thing to watch, Phee, and I was powerless to do anything, except have all the books ready."

"At home, we had Mary fighting for her life with each breath. Mary passed with consumption in October '88, just when the bankruptcy was being announced. Then two months later, mother died at forty-eight on the 29th December ..."

"I know this is painful – shall we call it a day?"

"It is painful, but I am doing this for Mother and Mary! We deserve the right to be heard!"

"We are probably nearly up to the accident anyway. Your father bought the *Presto* in June '88 and the *Frank Guy,* which of course he has been sailing ever since."

"Uncle, do you know who this Mrs François Vine is? There was a notice in the paper the other day saying that the ownership of the *Frank Guy* is in question."

"Euphemia, I cannot tell you; it is your father's private business. You will have to wait to ask him, dear, when he gets home.

Presto

I was rather taken aback by Uncle John but could tell there was no use saying any more. I decided to focus on the history lesson. "Uncle, I well remember running down that day to celebrate the new steel ship Father had bought half shares with Mr Anderson. I quietly snuck up on him that day to surprise him. I could see him standing back, mentally calculating the improvements he had to make to her. He looked prouder than a rooster at daybreak. After all he'd been through with the bankruptcy, we all needed something to celebrate! We had all been through so much that year, it was a bittersweet celebration.

"But, Phem, the *Presto* was a fine-looking ship of 338 tons bought from Captain Leidman of Sydney. I am so proud of the way your Father stood up to the bank and all his creditors. We have had such support from fellow highlanders. The banks had to finally agree to his proposal to trade on and pay his debts. Unfortunately, only six months ago, as you know, it had its bow stoved in when the steamer Ballinger collided into her and sank.

"*Presto* was leaking like a sieve. He had done well in four years to hold her, but I think with mounting debts he had had to relinquish ownership."

We both felt sore about the total wreck of the Waireka even though she was owned by Captain John Curran she was said in the papers to be 'The smartest three-masted intercolonial vessel trading out of the Waitemata'.

"When you build, design, and dream each night about bringing a ship to life, it always has a part of your heart. Ye see your father's in, boots 'n all. He does all the things he focuses on with heart; he wants perfection. He is a master craftsman first and a master mariner second. One of the toughest sailors ever to be on the sea yet loves his men with a passion.

"He cannot hide what he feels. You girls are his greatest delight!! and now you seven are all he has left and, of course, the *Frank Guy*.

"He is tenacious and at sixty-six, it has been like starting again."

"Uncle, he sometimes calls me 'Lassie' and quotes those lines in that broad Scottish accent:

> they that go down to the ships,
>
> that do business in great waters,
>
> these see the works of the Lord
>
> and his wonders in the deep …

"Uncle, if you were going to bring a history lesson to the children, what would you do it on?"

The Frank Guy

Chapter 16

Meeting John and Harry

My mind was overloaded with twenty-five years of activity: the labours, heartache, pain, bankruptcy, and storms Father had sailed through. I felt closer to him somehow, but something gnawed at me. In all the activity was something greater being lost. I had to clear my swimming head.

I looked across at the many ships in the harbour and altered my course as if drawn like a magnet to the docks. The cool wind softly caressed my hot forehead. I stood with my eyes closed, as it wafted like a feather across my face. I sat on a park bench watching muscle-bound workman slinging goods down into a hold, ropes hoisting crane loads of flax or bags of kauri gum onto a ship while a supervisor shouted over the noise. There were a few broke gum-diggers, demoralised from having spent all their earnings over the weekend – grieving loved ones parting forever to Europe – or welcomed back in a lover's embrace – expressmen vying for business – sailors mending sails and ropes. It was a pot of bubbling emotions of which I never tired.

As I passed by the other boatyards and ships, my heart was contemplative. *Will Father approve of me taking the place of Murdoch, the eldest son!? Am I ready to nurse Barbara when the time comes? Do I lay down my dream of independence and submit to a husband? Do I leave Father to manage his own household and be a modern businesswoman?*

I had been looking for a familiar face among the crowds boarding ships or milling about. I held mixed emotions at seeing Duncan too! I wanted to be held and kissed. *But if I surrender my heart, who will I become?* Deep in these thoughts, I could see a familiar young redhead. He stood back on at the stern of the steamer *Argyll*. It looked a lot like Duncan … Then I hesitated …

What am I doing? Did I really just call out his name?

The young man turned and leapt the rail onto the boarding plank; came towards me, smiling.

"Were you calling me? My name's John O'Flaherty."

"Oh, I am *so* sorry. I am Euphemia McQuarrie. You looked like a young man I know." Right then, I want to die of embarrassment.

"So, who is this fortunate fellow?"

I was blushing now. "He is a Shipwright's apprentice … to my Father, Captain Hector McQuarrie. He was working on repairs to a ship which had broken a mast in a storm. I thought I might catch sight of him."

Curses, why did I just tell him all that?

"Is he an Irishman?"

"He is from the Clan McKenzie of Nova Scotia, where my Mother Ann McLeod was born; he knew the McCleods well. He has kin up in Little Omaha. Anyway, I must be off. Good day." *The gaul of this man! Who does he think he is, asking me all these private questions?* I walked away but he started to skip along beside me.

"Miss McQuarrie, where are you from?"

"I do not know you, sir, and I do not think I need to tell you where I am from!"

"I am from Galway in Ireland, just across the sea, from clan

McKenzie. Well, if he looked like me, I think I like him already."

"You are nothing like him, sir. He has clear blue eyes." The muscles in my shoulders start to tighten.

"I think I have heard of your Father, Mr McQuarrie; from what I hear he is a fine captain!"

I turned a little to look over my shoulder. "I am sorry for the mix-up John but if I were a man, I would not have been harassed by you at all. Sometimes I wish I were a boy!"

"Well, Miss, pardon me saying, but I think that would be a sad mistake. You are far too pretty to ever be a boy."

"I have heard quite enough. I am leaving." Only then was I aware that another young man stood smiling at me as if we had met before somewhere. John turned around, seeing my interest.

"Oh, how rude of me. This is Harry!"

"Good afternoon, Miss. Did you say Hector McQuarrie?

"Yes. Have we met?"

"No, I do not think so. I would have remembered. However, I think I met your father in Wellington a few years back."

"Oh. How would you have met my father?"

"He was transforming a big three-masted ship into a steamer. I am trying to remember … the *Gailoch*? It was a few years ago now, but I remember because we played a friendly match with a few of his men from up this way. That is how we got acquainted with the boys from Parnell.

"You see, we have just arrived to play against Parnell on the 9th, Saturday morning.

"I am from Parnell and I had not heard there was a match being played. There are no lodgings up there anyway. Most of the boys are down in a local school hall. John, David and I are staying with a Mr and Mrs Petford. Apparently, they have a daughter Ruby about your age?"

"Yes, I do know of them, but it is a small community. I must be off now. All the best for your game."

"I am sorry if we upset you, Miss. It was just a bit of fun. Come to the game – it's at 10am Saturday, and we will make it up to you."

I stormed up the hill toward home but then decided to call on Ruby. Their mansion overlooks the harbour. *Who do those boys think they are, the arrogance of them both? How could they think any woman would be flattered?* I made my way to the back door where I could hear their two dogs barking. Rewa, the house girl, answered the door.

"Is Ruby home, Rewa?"

In a moment Ruby appeared. "Phee, I wasn't expecting you. Is everything alright? You will never guess who we have staying?"

By now I had calmed down a little, but my face was still flushed. "Could it be John O'Flaherty, Dave and Harry? Ruby, you will catch a fly with your mouth open. I think it is the first time I have ever seen you speechless."

"And what does that mean? How do you know about the rugby team coming through Father's lodge?"

"I met them down on the docks. I was so incensed I decided to come straight here. They were so rude to me."

"I can see your surprise!"

"I think you might have misunderstood them; they are fine young men. Isn't John simply charming?"

"Ruby, it has been a long day. You are my best friend so I will reserve my judgement before I say something I regret."

"Phee, don't be like that. Please come to the match. I need you as a chaperone to keep Father happy, and he does trust you!"

"I will think about it." I kissed her and made my way home. All the day's thoughts still reeled in my mind. In some ways, it was a crossroads and I did not know where to turn. I made my way back up the hill along Augustus Terrace to the house, deciding to put it out of my mind.

I normally struggled with the uphill climb to our house, but today my frustration carried me up the hill with ease. The dirt roads difficult in the shoes I wore, and I was glad to see the last stretch up to our corner. Our little community only had ten houses on our street. Parnell was like an island amongst the city of twenty-nine thousand. I had just arrived home and was removing my shoes, hat and sash when Bess suddenly started barking. Then there was a knock on the door.

I grabbed the porcelain knob, and there stood Aunt Christine. "Oh, good evening, Aunt. How wonderful to see you." Her face was pale; flooded with concern. "What is it, Aunt? It is quite late for you to call."

"I must speak to you privately!"

"Aunt Christine, what a surprise! Aunt Christine is here!" Maggie shouted out, flinging her arms about her.

"If I did not know better, I would think you are missing the Captain," said Aunt Christine.

Chapter 17

Storms on the Horizon

"Maggie, it is always a delight to see you. I love those red ribbons in your hair."

"I dressed up a little, any excuse! We are going to Eileen's for dinner. I am sure you could join us?"

"Please, Aunt!" Hannah bounced excitedly.

"Hannah, Maisy, I would like to, but I must get home to my own family for dinner. You boys behave yourself over there! Be polite, and you two, do not fight."

"What is this about?" A wave of fear went through my body, gripping my legs like a wild dog. "Is it Father? Are they shipwrecked?" *How would she know before me?* My mind was desperately tried to think what it could be.

"Let's talk in a few minutes. I will quickly help the girls do their hair. Put on the kettle." Christine barked orders at the children like a true ship's captain.

"Come on, boys. You need to get ready to go to Eileen's. Ken and Dug, you cannot go in shorts and bare feet. Go and get your long trousers and white shirt.

I quietly found Murdoch "Murdoch, you look lovely. Will you please help your brothers."

"Yes, Phee. Are you okay – you do not look well?"

"I'll be fine, Murdoch. I just need to prepare for Maggie's class next week. Could you help Maggie gather the children. It is almost 5pm."

"Aunt Christine is fussing over the girl's hair already. I will hurry the boys."

"Thank you, Murdoch."

I almost subconsciously poured milk into the sugar bowl as I prepared the tray. I put a cube of sugar in my cup to calm my nerves.

What could be in Father's sealed letter? I knew it couldn't be good: Christine had never come by so late before! Christine quickly tied a bow on Hannah's plaited hair. The children all came through.

"Oh, you all look beautiful! Well, done! Give Phem a kiss and off you go."

"Say goodbye to Aunt Christine too." The children excitedly swamped us both with hugs and kisses. "I will see you all in a few hours, around eight, Maggie!"

"Okay!" Maggie took Hannah's hand and the boys jostled each other out the door.

The house was finally quiet; Bess curled up again on her mat beside the fire.

I quickly poured the water into the teapot and put shortbread on a plate. "So, what is this hasty visit about?"

Christine picked up the tray. "Come, let's go to the sitting room."

I sat down. My chair was facing a photo of Mother and Father on the sideboard. I stared intently at Christine.

"I was reading the *Star* this afternoon and came across this article in the paper – I came as soon as I could get away. I was hoping you had not seen it, as I knew this is going to be a big shock."

Christine unfolded the article she had cut out of the

newspaper. My mind was preparing for a shipwreck of the *Frank Guy*, and I braced myself with every ounce of courage I could muster. It could be the only explanation of Father being so late on his return!

I trembled as I unfolded the small column; read quietly for a few seconds. "Oh my God! I don't understand! Can this be Father? They have spelt his name wrong, but he is the only master mariner who owns the *Frank Guy* and *Presto*. Surely this cannot be true! *Marriage!?*"

"Phee, I do not know. I thought for sure the Captain would have spoken of it with you and that perhaps you had kept it a secret! But I can tell by your shock, it is a complete surprise."

"A breach of promise, Aunt! It says:

In the supreme court yesterday before Justice Holroyd and a jury of six, action was brought by Pauline Francois to recover damages of £1000 from Hector McQuarrie, master mariner, in a breach of promise of marriage. A defence had been put in denying that any such promise had been made. But the defendant made no appearance in court.

"Phee, when would this have happened?"

"It says May 1892. A year ago. That was when the *Bellinger*, steaming into Port Melbourne from Tasmania in early May, cut across the bow of the *Presto* as she entered the harbour.

Bellinger went straight to the bottom. Father was not found to be at fault, but I seem to remember him saying he travelled to the owners in Sydney over the claim.

He was away for months, based in Melbourne. He would have also spoken directly to the insurance company as he likes to do business face to face.

"How would he have met her?"

"It says:

... they met on the steamer 'Elingmite' coming from Sydney to Melbourne early last year.

"I am guessing Father was returning to repair *Presto* and report to the Harbour Authority."

"But who is this Pauline Francios woman? Why is this the first time we have heard her name?"

"I do not know, Aunt, but a woman 'Francois Vine' placed an advert about two months ago, disputing the ownership status of the *Frank Guy!*"

"The article says that she normally went by the name 'Madame Vine'. Surely they are one and the same! Why would she have three different names?"

"The big question is, why would Father propose to somebody in such a hurry?"

"If he had gone through with it, you would now have a stepmother a few years older than Barbara!"

"It goes on to say that ...

they became intimately acquainted. Upon reaching Melbourne, they both stayed at the West Melbourne 'Coffee Palace', and afterwards at the 'Royal Hotel', Victoria Street. In May he appeared to have been struck by the fascinations of the widow, asked her to marry him, and she consented. With the usual impetuosity of a sailor, he was very anxious that it should come off as soon as possible.

"What rubbish! Father has never been impetuous in his life.

"A room and cake were ordered, and a date was

The Coffee Palace

"You are right, Christine. The bigger question is, how could
he consider marrying someone half his age?"

"They say,

The Captain was an old man, and she was a young woman.

"Father is sixty-seven. Why would he even consider marrying a woman half his age?"

"Have you seen the new Coffee Palace? I adore it! …"

The article said: they stayed and became "intimately acquainted" there. No! Intimately acquainted! … I scowled.

"… It literally looks like a palace. Gloriously extravagant! It is about nine storeys high running half a city street each way, on the corner of Collins Street. It is for those not wanting to drink or stay where people are intoxicated."

"The whole thing makes no sense at all!"

"I have read and re-read it myself in utter disbelief."

"Why would Father stay in such opulence?"

"I noticed at the end of the article it states that he said 'I am well to do'.

"A year ago, Aunt, he may have been 'well to do' and expecting the insurance payout for the *Presto*. He could not have imagined, only three months later, the *Frank Guy* would go aground and cost him more than his half share is even worth."

"I know, Phem, that you have had strict instructions to be careful with household spending."

"But, Christine, he ordered a cake, a ball, and a special dinner for all the guests! It says:

"He had a house in New Zealand that his daughter managed. Afterwards he told her however that Captain McKenzie had persuaded him not to marry a widow on account of his daughter."

"He has referred to Barbara of course, who at the time was managing the house and sacrificed her teaching career to nurse Mother and Mary."

"Perhaps a bigger sacrifice has been catching consumption off my sister, Annie, and losing her opportunity for marriage or a family."

"Surely Barbara must know!?"

"You would never get our Barb to divulge a secret though."

"It goes on to say that:

... three witnesses gave evidence! Mr McQuarrie had said she was his intended wife. The judge returned a verdict in ten minutes awarding £100 to her with costs."

"Why was it tried in the Supreme Court of Australia, without the Captain being able to attend?" Aunt Christine had flopped down on a chair.

"In a way, Father did give his defence, with lawyers on his behalf. That is why he left so early on 26 May to present his defence, hoping he could return on the 30th of August when the case was due to be heard. But he is still at sea."

"Surely, Phee, did he not say anything?!"

"Only now I realise he had seemed so broken. He had tried to tell me twice, but there were interruptions. He had also hugged me tightly, lingering slightly like he was trying to communicate something."

"It is late, I must get home to my family. We will not know the answer to many of these questions till the Captain returns. Pray he returns soon!"

I saw Aunt Christine out, already going over in my mind the conversations and details. The mantle clock had just chimed the half-hour — *where have those two hours disappeared.* I had to prepare for the children; put on makeup and brush my wild hair which was sticking up from my windswept walk home. I had to appear calm for the children's sake. Was it only three hours ago that I had disagreed with my best friend, who would embrace me and let me pour forth my heart — only now if it were possible?

I was still in shock. How could I contain this terrible secret? I could do nothing more but lock it up inside.

I decided to make a special treat for the children coming home to bed. I picked up the coal bucket and stoked the fire on the range to warm the house. I put a tablespoon of cocoa in a pot, with a dob of butter, ladled out the cream and poured it in with the milk and a few spoons of sugar. *Oh, I can see you, Mother, making hot chocolate, if only you were here now.* Bess jumped up just as the children burst through the door with excited chatter.

"I can tell you had a wonderful time! What did you have for dinner?"

"Shepherd's Pie with gravy and for dessert, sponge pudding."

"Eileen let me play with Rosie's doll. I dressed her in lovely dresses and hats. Rosie went to heaven!"

"That is lovely, Hannah, but I hope you did not say that in front of Eileen."

"No, she did not," said Maggie.

"If you're good, Hannah, I will let you go and visit another day. Come and sit down. I have made hot cocoa and you can have a shortbread biscuit." *I will try and put this whole wretched affair out of my mind for now.* "What did you boys do?"

"We played hide and seek; Ken hid behind the curtain and we could not find him anywhere!"

"This has been the best day ever!" said Hannah.

"No, it would be the best day ever if Father were home. Have you heard any word? I thought Aunt Christine looked like she might know something!"

"No, Murdoch, I haven't heard yet. When you have finished your cocoa, please get yourself off to bed. I will come and read a story if you come in your night clothes to Hannah's bed."

I tossed and turned all night, and finally slept in the early hours of morning. I woke to Hannah pulling faces in the mirror sitting at our dressing table. If only it had all been a dream and I could wake and be ten like Hannah, a time when Mother would sit me in front of the mirror and brush my hair. I dragged myself out of bed and gently brushed Hannah's.

I felt torn, Ruby wanted me to go to a meeting with her at ten. Perhaps if I went it would take my mind off things and I could get a chance to speak to her. But how could I avoid the subject of John O'Flaherty?

"Coo Wee, only me!"

"Oh, Aunt Christine! You did not have to come by; you have enough to deal with. Your timing is perfect though, I have just got all the children off to school."

"How are you? After last night I can see you did not sleep well."

"Of course … I worried all night about the *Frank Guy* being lost at sea or coming to grief. I had felt before Father left that something might happen to them. I am going to Captain McKenzie to see which ships have come in. See if he has any word and talk to him about this article.

"Surely he would let you know if he had any word?"

"If I know Captain McKenzie, he will tell only the facts and no 'if's' or 'possibilities'."

"Aunt, we have suffered humiliation over scandalous news reports, blaming us for the *Flying Cloud* disaster. Father's bankruptcy was plastered all over New Zealand's papers, and now this. Even if it is not true, our reputation is finished! People will not believe it to be lies."

"Euphemia McQuarrie, we are highlanders, proud to be from Clan McQuarrie, McLeod and McCallum. We have suffered our land being confiscated in the clearances; resettled in two countries and re-established houses and schools. We will weather this storm and survive. Life is certainly going to change for us all. Let me know how you go and I will see you later at the meeting.

Chapter 18

Message in a Bottle

I had only been to Captain McKenzie's house once when Father had asked me to deliver a letter to him. I put on my coat and made my way briskly up over the hill into the lower valley of Parnell. He had a generous home with white verandas bordered by wrought iron lacework along the roofline. I walked through the beautiful rose garden up to the front door.

"Mrs McKenzie came to the door. "Is the Captain in please, and is it convenient to see him?"

"Who shall I say is calling?"

"It is me, Mrs McKenzie, Euphemia!"

"Oh, dearie, my eyesight's not what it used to be. My, you are looking more like your Mother every day, bless her heart. I will just fetch him – come into the sitting room."

I sat looking at sketched black and white family portraits with gold frames – one of the Captain astride a handsome horse in full uniform as the Commander of the Rangitikei Cavalry. He had enlisted for the Maori wars. On one wall, a bookshelf neatly arranged with books on shipping, and a world globe that stood in pride of place on a small separate table. The most curious thing was a large map on the wall showed Australia, Caledonia, Fiji, Noumea, and New Zealand with the Pacific Ocean. It had dressmaking pins with tiny red flags with coordinates written on them.

"Euphemia, lovely to see you, my dear! You are wondering what my map is about? For many years now, I have set adrift in the ocean 108 bottles with notes inside as a study of sea currents. I always give the coordinates and ask the discoverer to let me know where they have been found. Last week I received my first returned bottle. It was discovered on the Kaipara heads on August 9th having travelled some 300 miles.

"Oh my! That is most fascinating. Do you include any personal information?"

"Heavens no, just the ship and captain. However, I think you are here on another matter. I can already guess … is it about your father?"

"Was it you who advised my father not to marry Madame Vine? How did you come to be there?"

"Please take a seat, dear. I had called into Melbourne on the way back from Noumea in the brigantine *Eillan Donan* when I met Captain McQuarrie at the port. He was most desirous for us to meet and consider ideas over what options he had concerning the wreck *Presto*. We agreed to meet later in the day in the Coffee Palace and take tea together to talk about her repairs. He seemed in fine spirits under the circumstances. I must confess, I was busy preparing to leave in a few days' to return to Auckland. But as you know, we have been good friends now going back to the building of the *Flying Cloud*.

"He had discovered the *Presto* was going to be expensive to fix, being a steel ship with its bow stoved in. I advised him to sell her as a wreck and retire.

"However, he then asked me with great delight if I would consider coming as a good friend and attend his wedding, which was to be in a few days. I can say I was quite gasping for air. I had not seen the Captain so excited for many a year. At first, I did not know what to say. He is a passionate man at the best of times, but he was like a young lad again. I chose to be most delighted for him and enquired as to the lucky lady. He explained they had only met on the ship *Elingmite* coming from Sydney a week ago and how he had not felt this way in so many years. He spoke of his grief at losing four children and two wives, including his first daughter Mary at seventeen, and Margaret, in Mull, the *Flying Cloud* debacle, bankruptcy and then his Annie five years ago. I can tell you as you get old, my dear, it can be one loss after another. Your bones ache, everything is harder, slower and you start preparing for the grave. Your mind still thinks you're eighteen, but your body will just not follow. Even wise old men can be bewitched.

"Mr McKenzie, I have only known Father to be full-on! Passionate and driven. But I have been on the *Frank Guy* a few times lately and his knees are going. He comes alive at sea, sailing instinctively but his heart is broken having lost so much."

"Well, lass, he insisted on me coming to the dinner celebration and ball. I agreed to change my plans and stand next to him on the day as his best man. Later that evening, I met Mrs Vine. She was dressed in the most seductive red dress, bonnet, scarf and matching handbag of the highest quality. She was beguiling. She removed her glove and offered her hand as the Captain announced 'this is my wife to be'."

"I do not understand Mr McKenzie why the wedding had to happen so quickly. They could have waited."

"Well, I think she put pressure on him because she had offered to help him financially to repair the *Presto* but would only invest in it once they were married. After our pleasantries, I asked her a little about herself, but something about her answers did not seem right. I have met a thousand people over the years, you just get a feeling."

"So, what did you do?"

"What could I do? I found the timetable for the *Elingmite* and it was due in harbour the next day. I went down there promptly, and her Captain was extremely informative. He said she was well known now but had come from South Australia where she had been in trouble. This time she had absconded to Hong Kong after swindling £429 off a poor fellow. Instead of selling tobacco, she was illegally selling wine and other things I wish not to mention.

"A policeman, Mr Stokes, tracked her down in Hong Kong after her skipping bail on a 12-month jail sentence. She is cunning and eluded him with her many wiles. After many weeks undercover he finally returned her aboard the *Elingmite* to Melbourne. Unfortunately, your father just happened to be aboard and succumbed to her charm, thinking her to be a poor widow of significant means, she thinking he was an easy target to swindle."

"Who were the three witnesses 'Madame Vine' had testify on her behalf."

"I only got to see one of her so-called friends, but they were not people of good character. I returned to your father, sat him down and relayed to him the whole sordid tale.

"He was in shock, to say the least. Whatever brokenness he had experienced was now doubled. I did worry for his life!"

"Poor Father! I cannot believe a woman could be so cruel!"

"Your Father still had weeks of work to sort out concerning the *Presto*, so he checked out of the Coffee Palace immediately and moved to the Royal Hotel. She, however, found him and accosted him about running out on the proposal."

"Why do you think he said his daughters would not approve?"

"He was desperate to come up with a plausible reason. He had no choice *but* to say that his daughters would not approve.

"She became enraged and said she would take it to the highest court. He tried to offer her compensation once the *Presto's* claim was settled but she wanted more.

"He had no choice but to sell the *Presto* as a wreck, as his whole financial situation was unravelling in front of his eyes.

"What is to become of us now, Captain?"

"Your father is a resilient man. However, he had only a small hope to recover by running day and night fully loaded to Australia and back.

"The *Frank Guy* is his only hope. I am not sure how he can possibly recover this time after her going ashore at Woolgoolga."

"I am so sorry, Euphemia. I offered to go and represent him in Melbourne, but he insisted he would fight it himself.

"He knew the case was coming up, sailing in plenty of time to set up his defence in Melbourne and return before the 30th August. Has there been any word of his passage?"

"No. We have heard nothing!" I rose to my feet as strength filled my body. "As God is my witness, Captain, have you any word at all?" I stood almost in defiance, mustering all my courage.

"Miss McQuarrie, I believe you are as tough and courageous as your father. Out of respect to him, and you, I will tell you all I know. I have been asking for weeks now, and the only report I have is of a ship called the *S.S. Matatua* which was steaming toward Wellington from Lyttleton when she got caught in a terrible storm and driven out to sea. The captain thinks he caught sight of the *Frank Guy* headed on a course away from Wellington. She must have been in trouble as she was not under sail and waves were breaking over her."

I gasped, and my legs suddenly turned to jelly. The courage I thought I had suddenly drained out of me like pulling a bath plug. I sat down again, feeling faint.

"Mrs McKenzie came in with a tray of hot scones and tea. She rushed over to me.

"Oh, my dear girl, are you alright." She went off and came back with a wet cloth for my forehead.

"It has been a very eventful few days. I am distressed about Father's whereabouts."

"It is our cross to bear, dear, those left behind always worrying about loved ones at sea."

"I do not know which is worse … finding out about this scandal or worrying that Father has perished. I should feel relieved about the explanation of Father's marriage proposal, but I feel sick and powerless now waiting for him to return. How am I going to face him?"

"Euphemia, my dear, he needs your grace, forgiveness and support like never before. Treat him like he has been saved from the sea to live again."

I numbly stared at her as I rose to my feet, thanking them for their kindness.

Mrs McKenzie asked about the children, their schooling and Barbara before giving me a motherly hug as I went out the door.

Chapter 19

Christian Women's Temperance

I rushed back to the house. It was already 2pm and our meeting with the Woman's Christian Temperance Union was at three. I went straight to the front porch to look out to the harbour. *I cannot spend the next few days, weeks, waiting for the house flag of the Frank Guy to come into view. I must try and give the illusion that everything is fine. On Sunday we will go to church and I will pretend I know nothing of the ensuing storm about to hit our beautiful home.*

I rushed about the house doing chores; changed into a warm dress after a wash. I pulled out my special mauve hat that matched the sash on my white pleated dress, and was trying to manage my wild hair when Ruby came through the front veranda door.

"Phem, are you there? "

"Is that you, Ruby? In here! Come through."

"There you are – you did get ready! You look delightful! I love your matching sash and shoes. Are you going to wear this matching hat? Let me help you with your hair."

I sat at the dressing table and spoke to Ruby in the reflection of the mirror.

"How do you want it? I think it might look nice in a bun with the hat pinned on top.

"That would be wonderful!" As she carefully brushed then gathered my hair together, I caught her eye. "Ruby …!?"

"Yes."

"Would we still be friends if I married someone who was poor?"

"What a thing to ask me! Of course, we would! Look at me … I am infatuated with poor Mr John O'Flaherty!"

Ruby pulled my hair a little tighter. "What about if I was shunned by society for something I did not do?"

Ruby slipped the final pin through my bun and hesitated for a second. "Where is this all coming from? Have you done something naughty! I am glad I came early now. I did not realise it would be so interesting."

"I want to apologise for my behaviour yesterday afternoon; it was uncalled for."

"I cannot believe it – are you ill? I will accept your apology before you retract it. In fact, I was not being very kind either … Is everything alright, Phem? You have not got pregnant, have you?"

I just stared in silence at her reflection with annoyance. "Can you get that button at the back of my dress for me please!"

"Hold still … there! Phee, what if I wanted to marry a poor man?"

"What?"

"Father and mother have been trying to match me with this lawyer from Sydney. He came here to settle disputes arising from gold claims. He is also in Father's lodge. He is thirty-eight and now owns a house in town. I want to marry someone who is carefree and more my age, not fourteen years older!"

"My parents had almost that gap and were really happy. But what is all this about?"

She came round to look at me, face to face, and said, "I want to be in love. I want to giggle and laugh like I do with John."

"Ruby, you are spoilt and privileged. You need your Father's help financially and the status that brings. Can you really imagine being poor? You have never been poor!"

"Euphemia! What has gotten into you? I have never known you to speak to me like this."

"Sorry, Ruby, I have a lot on my mind. Let us just get on our way, I think it is nearly time. I have things to tell you, but we have no time now."

There was plenty of excited voices as we came to the door of the local hall. We were welcomed at the door and surprised to see so many women at a temperance meeting. Immediately I saw Aunt Christine, and Sarah, who waved to us. They had kept two seats for us. We each hugged and took our seats. "You remember Ruby?"

"Of course, we do – lovely to see you again. You both look delightful, Phee. I like your hair!"

She looked at me knowingly, so as not to hint at our secret. "Thank you, Aunt!"

"Welcome, ladies, let us get started. Please settle down – you are extremely excited today and will get a chance to speak to each other later. I can see that we have almost double the number of women here today that we had last meeting – it is fortunate that we have enough chairs. As we meet, there are ladies meeting in many places … Grafton, Northshore and so. We are excited by events that are unfolding. For those of you who have not been here before – Welcome! I will recap for those who are not sure about what we stand for.

"The WCTU was primarily set up more than twenty years ago to highlight woman's suffrage as a means to fight liquor prohibition. But it has become much more as ladies all over New Zealand and the world are letting their voices be heard.

Kate Sheppard, who has been one of the most vocal activists for our movement, has said: *"We are tired of having a "sphere" doled out to us, and of being told that anything outside that sphere is unwomanly."*

"Over the past three years, we have lobbied the government by signing petitions asking for women to have the right to vote. In 1891, 1892 and now, 1893, the House of Representatives passed the bill that grants the vote to adult women again, but in the Upper House it had foundered.

"It has been all about the men thinking we would advocate for there to be prohibition, but 25,000 women who signed this last petition are just wanting equal rights for women. That is why we have been on the streets campaigning to bring about change. If this bill is passed in a few days' time, we will be the first country in the world to have women over twenty-one being able to vote.

"Raise your hand please if you are just old enough to vote! Oh, quite a few of you. How would it feel for you to cast your vote in the first election? …"

"Ruby, can you imagine us being able to cast our vote!"

"Phee, I hate to think what Father would say! But he does not even need to know I have voted if I go to another polling station. They are setting up four voting stations again. He likes to vote at the Parnell Hall. I will vote at Haslett's Hall on Eden Terrace."

"Good for you!" we whispered.

"This is the first of many measures we wish to bring in. Ladies, we need you to sign up to tennis clubs, golf courses. If you are interested, we already have a local croquet club… the vote will again reach the Upper House almost as we speak. We are praying for a miracle!"

The murmuring was so loud the speaker had to stop.

"Ladies! Ladies! I agree, but I will be finished in a few minutes. Thank you! Richard Seddon, as you know, is opposing the bill being passed and will do all he can to sabotage it. We need twenty votes to get it through. Ladies, if that happens, in just weeks we will be able to go to the polls and make our vote count for the first time in history in an election. The elections are being held on the last week in November, so get the word out there, ask every woman you know to go to the polls and be heard. We are some of 307,000 women's voices in New Zealand today!"

The atmosphere was electric. "I have never been in a group of ladies that are so excited."

We stayed afterwards for tea and cake, filled with a new hope and vigour. I had not realised what a dark cloud I had been under waiting for Father to come home. When I arrived home, all the children were already home, the boys hanging about the larder for something to eat.

"Where were you, Phee? We looked all over the house!"

"I have been out at a meeting with the WCTU. It is unusual for you to come home and I am not there. Perhaps you will have to get used to it."

Ken asked, "Why? Have you got a cleaning job or something? Anyway, what is WCTU?"

"Cleaning work is not all that women can get employment doing, you know. One day women might be lawyers and politicians, maybe even a Prime Minister. I can see I am going to have to educate you boys a little. WCTU is a group of women who are standing up for equal rights in New Zealand."

"A woman could never be Prime Minister!"

"What would you know, Dug," Maggie said.

"I do not understand – don't women already have rights for things?"

"Dug, I know it is hard for you to understand, but imagine you went to play football and only girls were allowed to play – you wanted a horse but only girls were allowed to ride horses. What about church? Only women could speak – a restaurant and only women were allowed in! That is what it is like for us now. We cannot vote for a Prime Minister, step into a men's club, become Mayor of a city, play in any men's sports, speak in church."

"Our youth leader at the church says it is devilish to have women taking men's roles."

"*Oh*, does he! Interesting! Here, Dug, would you like a sandwich? Here is the bread, now make one for everyone, including Murdoch, who is studying in his room! I will have corned brisket on mine with mustard. Thank you."

I turned and walked off without looking back.

"Phee, what do you mean? I do not know how to cut the bread or where to find anything!"

I shouted out, "Looks like a good opportunity to learn!"

Chapter 20

Women Win the Right to Vote

Two more days came and went, but in the afternoon of the 8th, I went specially to the corner store to get the evening news. There, emblazoned across the front page, was the bold heading: WOMEN WIN RIGHT TO VOTE! I could hardly believe my eyes. I bought an extra copy and ran down the hill to Ruby's house. Almost out of breath, I blurted out, "Ruby! Ruby!"

I could hear her not so delicate steps all the way down the hall. She flung open the door!

"Phem, what is it?"

"Look!" I held up the front page and shouted, "WE ARE GOING TO BE THE FIRST WOMEN TO VOTE!"

Ruby threw her hand over her mouth. And squealed with delight. "Really! What does it say?"

We laughed. "I do not know yet. I just came straight here to tell you!" We turned the page to read.

Seddon Opposed the bill unlike many of the liberals whose women folk supported prohibition. Seddon had expected to stop the bill in the upper house but found that one more vote was needed. Thomas Kelly, a new liberal Party councillor had left himself paired in favour of the measure, but Seddon obtained his consent by wire to change his vote.

"Oh, how exciting!! Yehah!" In all our excitement, we had not noticed the three football billets standing watching us. Ruby turned and giggled.

"This, gentlemen, is my best friend, Euphemia McQuarrie!"

John just stood there speechless, looking at me, but Harry stepped forward straight away and put forth his hand, and said, "Miss, it is a pleasure to meet you!"

He had a twinkle, almost like a gentle giggle in his blue eyes. Why had I not noticed how handsome he was before! "Oh, how lovely to meet you!" Even I was shocked at my own reaction. *Get hold of yourself*, I told myself sternly.

"I would just like the opportunity to apologise for the other day. I felt so bad afterwards, I had thought of coming to ask your forgiveness. My friend is Irish — what more is there to say — he is rude, uncourteous and inconsiderate! Could we please start again? Have you had word of your father?"

He put his arm around John, who picked up on the hint and snapped a rose off the nearest bush and offered it to me.

"Thank you, John. My father is not in yet … thank you for asking! I would also like to apologise, as I have not been myself lately and quite rude. Ruby will attest to that."

"Yes, she has been quite forthright this week. Come inside, everyone, I think we must celebrate and put this behind us. Father, we will use the garden seats?"

Mr Petford came round the corner from his drawing-room.

"Good afternoon, all. How nice to see you, Euphemia. Ruby tells me your father is still not in port!"

"Good afternoon, Mr Petford. Sorry for the shouting: we were just celebrating the bill being passed for the women's vote. Isn't it wonderful!"

Ruby was standing behind her father, making big eyes and winking at me to get my attention.

"Well, all I can say is, thank God that is over. We can get on with things, and hopefully that will be the last we hear of it."

I could feel the hairs on the back of my neck bristle. I was about to launch into a speech about it just being the start of women's rights in New Zealand, but just as I took a breath, Ruby grabbed my arm firmly and dragged me involuntarily toward the kitchen.

"Father, we will be in the kitchen. Can we make you tea?"

"No, thank you. It is already quarter past three. I will wait for dinner now."

We sat in the back garden while Rewa made tea for us all.

"How do you like your visit so far?"

"It is a fine city, a world away from Wellington and all that politics. I am so glad to see women finally get the right to vote – it is high time women had equal rights. My mother has scraped by for years with eight of us to feed, all on her own.

"Every time she would ask for help, she was asked to bring her husband in. She had no right to own property or earn a decent wage, so we all had to go and get work at an early age. At ten years old I was stacking hay for the neighbours and getting up at four to milk."

"What happened to your father?"

"He was kicked in the head by a horse and he has been in a mental asylum ever since."

"Oh, that is so sad. And your Mother? How has she managed?"

She moved up to Martinborough recently. The youngest are in secondary school now. We do not see a lot of them, but my brother James goes over the hill quite often."

"What do you do?"

"Oh, I was a cabbie till last year when I decided to take a job with a Livery agent. We buy and sell horses, train them, race them, and breed good stock. How long has the Captain been away now?"

"He left 26th of May, nearly four months ago! I was expecting him mid-July. I know he is my father, but many people will tell you he is one of the safest master mariners on the sea. I cannot recall him ever having a mishap where he is to blame. I am trying not to think of it as I can do nothing and must stay strong for the children."

Harry had been most attentive, looking me straight in the eyes and watching my mouth as I spoke.

"Ruby told me a little about you when I asked after you the other day. She said you are managing the whole house, full time. It must be a big responsibility. I am sorry you lost your mother at such a young age; you must miss her terribly."

I could feel a lump rising in my throat. How was it this stranger understood my struggle? I was not about to collapse into a blubbering mess on the floor, but even when Ruby, my best friend was listening to me, it felt like she was not fully there. It felt so natural to talk to him, like we had known each other for years. I had almost forgotten – it was Friday night, when the children do an easy meal. "I am sorry Harry, but I must get home to the children. We will come to the game tomorrow and hope Parnell beats you boys from Wellington!"

"We will do our best to let them win, Miss."

We both laughed. "Harry, please call me Euphemia. Or

most people call me Phem or Phee."

"Euphemia, what do you *like* to be called."

"Euphemia is fine, thank you."

Ruby had been deep in conversation with John, and I had to go and tap her on the shoulder. "See you tomorrow, Ruby. It has been the loveliest afternoon. I will see you about 9:30." She jumped up and gave me a hug.

"I am so happy you will come."

She waved me off at the door.

Chapter 21

Wellington Versus Parnell

Saturday was slightly windy with squalls of rain; it was most unpleasant, but I had been in worse out at sea. There was still no sign of Father so I put on a heavy dress, took a blanket and asked the children if they wanted to see the game. Presently Ruby arrived with her driver and all the boys squeezed in as we headed over to Epsom. We sheltered behind a tree at Potter's paddock and could just see the action from our vantage. Despite the weather, about 500 people were spectating in warm coats. The players were warming up, passing the ball back and forth, sprinting laps across the field.

Harry was taller than most of the other men; he tossed the ball in the air and winked at me for a second. Wellington won the toss and the ball was kicked off from Parnell's end. I had cheered a few times for Parnell but my heart was really cheering for Harry. He was a fine player, skilful and quick; generous in setting up the ball for another player. Parnell made no headway in the scrum, with John and Harry locked together. Their legs were like iron posts, backs rippling with strong muscles. Harry told me he had wrestled often with his brother and made £5 a few times in Thames. They played like one man passing the ball out of the forwards to the wing. They took the ball at centre, with lightning speed charged down, carrying the ball to the opponent's line. Harry threw himself over the line at the left corner flag for a touchdown. We all clapped and got a little too excited. Harry looked our way and smiled while doing a slight bow.

"Did you see that, Murdoch? That guy looked at us and bowed. Do you know him?"

"He is staying at Ruby's with two other men."

It was an exhilarating game, and at full-time Wellington had won 7 points to 0. I know we should have been sad, but Harry and John had played well. We ran to the sideline and congratulated them. "Well done! You play a good game. Why don't you see if you can play for New Zealand in black jerseys."

Harry laughed, still catching his breath. John spoke up in his Irish accent. "Miss, we are not that serious; it is just a bit of fun. Come and join us with the boys for some cake."

"I am sorry, but we really must get back home; we are wet and I want to spring-clean the house before Barbara comes home. If the dusting is not done, she will be most displeased. Please come to the house for afternoon tea. I would be most happy if you could come."

Harry glanced at John and Ruby to judge their approval. "We would like that; we will see you at 4."

We arrived home, and I looked at the messy house as if through Barbara's eyes. I had not noticed how untidy it had become. I called out, "Get changed and come as quickly as you can."

Maggie and Maisy had gathered the children to sit down at the table. "I believe Father and Barbara could be home any day. It is already spring, and we need to spring clean the house from top to bottom like Barbara would. Maggie, could you please gather up all the washing, strip the sheets off the beds and put on the copper for hot water – you can use the bath to soak a few things. Murdoch, I need you to roll up the floor rugs, brush and shake them out.

"Ken and Dug, take turns to split wood and fill up the wood boxes in each room and fill up the coal buckets. There is no time for any play today but, if you behave, I will make toffee later. Hannah, please take a damp rag and dust all the shelves and ornaments starting in the sitting room. We have two hours, then we have guests arriving with Ruby."

I started in the bedrooms, tidying dolls and toys away, putting books into shelves, and re-making all the beds. The children were surprisingly focused, perhaps in anticipation of finally having Father home.

I quickly threw together a double batch of scones and stoked up the firebox. I put two small trays in and refilled the kettle while glancing at the clock in the lounge –a quarter to four. I ran about seeing how each of the children had progressed and was most proud of their efforts. I shouted out, "On the chime of four, stop and we will have hot scones!"

I arranged the table with a fresh cloth and linen serviettes, Mother's china and her silver cutlery. I had roughly cut the scones square and they had risen perfectly, bulging into each other, golden brown with a few on the edge overdone. I cast the last two trays in the oven and arranged Blackberry jam and fresh cream in two bowls just as the clock chimed. I filled a pot with milk and put it on the stove just as the children all came running, hungry from their chores and being in the cold wind that morning.

"Take a plate and two scones to the lounge. I will bring a jug of warm milk – please try not to make a mess. Maggie, could you please stir the milk for me while I run and get changed."

I had just stepped out of my dress when Bess started barking. "Murdoch, could you please get the door!" I had no time to pretty myself, so put on a red scarf, and put on my white crinoline dress. Suddenly I remembered the scones and rushed to the kitchen. There was a little smoke as I thrust open the steel door. "Bother!" Only a few in the centre of the tray were ok. Harry came through and tried to distract the conversation away from my folly.

"It's turning out to be a lovely afternoon now the sun has broken through the clouds. "

I had made up the table on the front porch and Murdoch politely introduced himself and the other children.

"You were the player who bowed after that try!"

Harry laughed. "Do you play? You look strong Murdoch. Who do you play for?"

"Just my local under-fifteens here in Parnell; most of the boys are from our school."

"I started playing at school in Timaru myself, and all my brothers."

As Harry turned, I was surprised at my nervousness. I was almost a little too chatty when I became nervous. "I am sorry about the smoke, please help yourself."

Ruby quietly put her hand on my shoulder, knowing I was about to make a fool of myself. I noticed Harry disappear into the kitchen, coming back with two burnt scones.

"I am hungry. These scones smell so great!"

"Oh, please, Harry don't eat those — they are burnt! There are plenty of scones."

"These remind me of my sister's scones, I always love them a little charred." He looked up and smiled, and I decided to take it with the generosity that was intended.

"The place looks lovely. Barbara will be most impressed, I assure you."

"Thank you, Ruby. The children have worked hard. Please come and have the scones while they are hot." A light breeze was blowing but not enough to make it unpleasant. A few sailing ships were racing in the harbour and it looked pretty to see all the sails.

I kept catching Harry's eye as he sat looking out to sea. He smiled once or twice then lifted his chair in one hand and sat next to me. I could not help but notice Maggie watching our every move.

"So Harry, who are you going to vote for?"

"Oh, I am not old enough to vote yet for another year. What about you?"

"I have not yet decided, but I do think our local candidate has represented Parnell well. What day are you off home?"

"We must leave Monday, but we are coming to church with you both tomorrow."

I could not believe how good it felt to have an adult conversation and someone interested in my world. Harry was also good with the children, teasing the boys and flirting with the girls a little. He came and helped me in the kitchen, and we had leftover cold lamb and a pot of potatoes in butter. In no time, our guests had to leave. I had not thought of Madame Vine once in four hours. It was Sunday tomorrow, and I was not sure how folk would respond to Father's news, but tonight, I did not have a care, for my heart was full of a warm glow I had not felt before.

At first light, I could hear the boys out on the veranda looking out to sea. It had become our routine, searching diligently for the *Frank Guy's* mast.

I was hoping everyone would be understanding about Father's indiscretion. Most were likely thinking about the elections, which were happening in six weeks. I asked Maggie to help get the children dressed, and Murdoch to help with the two boys. I was ironing Maggie's dress and the boys' white shirts. I had so much to tell Aunt Christine but how to talk to her in private.

It seemed a long walk up the hill to church, but I felt proud of our beautiful family. Reverend was standing outside greeting people as they entered.

"Euphemia, how are you? I have heard that your father is not home yet. We are praying for his eminent return!"

"Thank you, Reverend. I have been keeping busy to take my mind off it." We took our usual seats halfway down the left-hand side of the church. I loved to gaze high up into the beams of the church ceiling at the beautiful craftsmanship done by all the Nova Scotian carpenters and shipwrights.

I was not looking forward to questions about Father's absence. It took my mind off everything, thinking that I might see Harry if Ruby had managed to bring them along. I had smiled at a few folks and waved at Aunt Sarah. The oddest thing happened when I caught Uncle John's McQuarrie's eye: he purposely looked away. A few other folks had not acknowledged they had seen me – perhaps they had things on their minds too. I could now see Ruby two rows ahead sitting next to John and Harry. They both looked dashing in their suits. My heart gave a little flutter.

Chapter 22

Bigotry and Judgments

It seemed the hymns were particularly hearty that morning before the Reverend got up to speak. I could not concentrate properly as I kept looking at Harry sitting just a few rows in front.

"As you know, it will soon be the elections, and we must congratulate the women for the bill that was passed only a few days ago.

There was suddenly lots of murmuring in the congregation.

"I wish to speak today about Judgement. And my reading comes from a well-known passage in Matthew 7. I have asked young Hector, John McQuarrie's son to bring the reading this morning.

Hector was dressed in fine clothes with his hair swept back. He opened the Reverend's big bible and, finding the verse he read:

"Judge not, that ye be not judged. For with what judgement ye judge, ye shall be judged: and with what ye mete, it shall be measured to you again. And why beholdest thou the mote that is in thy brother's eye, but considerest not the beam that is in thine own eye. Thou hypocrite, first cast out the beam out of thine own eye; and then shalt thou see clearly to cast out the mote out of thy brother's eye."

"Thank you, Hector. Well done. In life, we often come across circumstances where someone has done something, and we are appalled by it. We feel we are so justly able to judge them for their behaviour. I think of the women caught in adultery that was about to be stoned. Can you actually imagine taking stones and throwing them at a person standing right in front of you? Perhaps their skull is even crushed as they bleed to death in front of you. It is a horrific thought."

People squirmed in their seats.

"The bible tells us that Jesus came along and wrote on the ground. Have you ever considered what he wrote in the dust that day? We can all think of huge wrongs like adultery, stealing, killing. I think maybe he wrote things like gossip, hate, anger, greed, unkind words, pride, lying, all the things we also suffer from that do not seem so terrible. It says, one by one from the oldest first, everyone left until she stood with no one to accuse her.

"My message today is, if there is a brother among us who has fallen, remember we all have failings of our own. With the judgement we judge, we shall also be judged."

I had put my head down a number of times – it was as if he was speaking to me! Each time I looked up again, someone else was looking my way with a furtive glance. Surely, it was only in my imagination. What did Father's love affair have to do with me? I could not help it; I became more and more uncomfortable until I just got up and walked out to the lady's bathroom. I splashed my face with a little water when I became aware of two other ladies in the cubicles talking. I could have sworn I heard two older ladies use Father's name. I stopped to listen.

"Oh, yes, he's a fine young lad that Hector – as you say he did well with that reading. Not like the other Hector. I would never have thought him to run off with some young girl half his age. What was he thinking!"

"I agree. To ask the poor girl to marry him, invite everyone then not even show up for the wedding, it is despicable! I think he deserves all he gets."

"I think he got off lightly with only £100. He might have to sell his house to pay for it now."

I stood in utter disbelief, so outraged I could not help myself.

"It is absolutely disgraceful! How dare you talk about my father that way! The woman was a swindler and a liar."

One of the ladies, Mrs Shaw, came out of her cubicle, straightening her dress.

"I hope you're not addressing me, lass. You ought to be ashamed."

"No. It is not *I* who should be ashamed but *you*! To think my father has shown good character all these years and for one misdemeanour you stone him!"

"You just wait a minute, lass! Don't you get high and mighty with me! Your Father deserves to be bankrupt for this. Consider what shame he has brought on our good names."

I could take no more. I was holding a wet towel and before I could think clearly, I threw it at her face knocking her bonnet off her head and into the sink. As I walked out, I heard loud shrieks which could be clearly heard inside the church. I had taken three steps toward my seat when the whole congregation turned to look at the commotion. I froze as folk now started to sneer and murmur. I turned and ran out the door.

I sat for a minute on a low stone wall, unsure whether to wait for the children or go home. Ruby, John, and Harry burst through the vestry door. Clutching Ruby, I wept, sobbing from deep in my soul.

"Phee, I know you will want to wait for the children, but I

will wait and bring them home. Harry, would you mind walking Euphemia to her house? I insist."

Harry had taken a handkerchief out of his pocket and handed it to me. He never said a word but quietly lay his jacket across my shoulders. "Thank you so much!"

"Give me a minute, Euphemia."

He ran back and caught Ruby on the steps and whispered something in her ear, to which she nodded.

He came back and asked if I would like to go for a ride. As he said it, he skillfully unhitched the sulky rope, patted the black mare affectionately and waved for me to come. He helped me into the seat and swung us around; headed back down the steep hill. "How will Ruby and John get home?"

"They will walk the children back; it was a squeeze with three in the seat coming anyway."

He deftly held the reins, years of experience with horses and carts as a cabbie evident. We turned right at the bottom of the hill and made our way along the shore. It felt wonderful to have the sea breeze in my hair and the light swish of waves on the sand. He eased back the reins and we stopped in a little grass area where the sun glistened like diamonds on the ocean. We were not far from Father's old shipyard, and perhaps I had him on my mind, but I suddenly blurted out:

"It is Father. He proposed marriage to a woman half his age in Melbourne and then ran out before the ceremony!"

Harry said nothing but listened intently.

"I feel angry with him for tarnishing our reputation. He is at sea, and we are the ones who are stained and soiled by his indiscretion. Who will ever marry me now my father is Hector McQuarrie, the "inconstant sailor?" That is the title of the article, it could not be further from the truth. Who will ever believe the truth now? That woman, Mrs Shaw, almost cursed my father. How could she be so cruel? How could God have done this to us? – perhaps we are cursed! What will Ruby think when she finds out?"

"It will pass. It will take time, but no one will ever write a book about this. You will marry one day, and those who love you will still feel the same way, and those who respected Hector will still respect him. We are all human. Ruby already knows about the article; her father brought it to her. All she said was 'Good on you, Hector!' to her father's dismay.

"You are blessed to have a father who is so resourceful. My mother was shunned by everyone because we were poor. We would not give our address out because we lived in a poor area of town. My clothes were all-hand-me-downs from other kids, so I always make sure I have nice clothes to wear. Mother took in lodgers that had nowhere else to go – alcoholics, suicidals – we have seen them all. My school years were dogged by kids at school teasing me about my dad being a 'lune', so I ended up in quite a few fights!"

"Oh, Harry, my father also came from a poor family with eight children in Mull – they almost starved. This has driven him to work himself almost to death. We have lived really well, but he has either been at sea or at work. Harry, I do not want to be poor, but I fear for Father's business. I thought if I could learn the business that I could take it over someday, but will there be anything left to manage?"

"Euphemia, you are a strong, beautiful woman; one day you will have your own business. You may even look back and laugh at throwing a towel at a lady's head. You may look back forty years from now, with grandchildren in your arms, celebrating being one of the first women to vote."

He had just spoken life into my soul. I looked into his handsome face, and his eyes sparkled like the water. His strong hand took mine, helping me into the carriage. I could not believe I had shared my heart with a stranger – it was like we were destined to meet. I wanted to be bathed in his warmth, wrapped in his arms.

"Come, I must get you back home; the children will wonder where you are!"

"I am dreading facing the children. I have now ensured that the folk at church consider us the laughing stock of the community."

"I think you could be surprised; they might understand better than you think."

He dropped me to the door and took my hand. "Euphemia, I must leave tomorrow, but this has been a special time that I will hold dear till we meet again." He kissed me gently on the cheek, then leapt in one movement onto the cart. He swung the horse around, calling out as he disappeared up the hill. "I will write!"

It was not till he had gone that I noticed shouting and noise inside the house.

Bess was barking as I opened the door. I almost fell over the trunk in the hall. For a second, I froze, disbelieving that it could possibly be true. *Father!*

I ran to the porch where the children were sitting enthralled by a story that Father had already launched into. He rose to his feet; threw his arms around me.

"Oh, lass, how wonderful to see you. It is like waking from the sweetest dream, only I am not dreaming!"

We held each other and I did not want to let go. All my rage had gone in that one moment.

Chapter 23

Father's Bittersweet Return

I held Father tight but wondered at the wrath that might come once he discovered what I had done.

"Where have you been?" Barbara appeared from the kitchen holding up one of my charred scones, a grin on her face. I was shocked to see such great colour in her skin and she had put on a tiny bit more weight.

"That is the only scone left from a double batch. I assure you I was not feeding the children burnt food."

She came up with the most affection she could muster and swished a cotton thread off my shoulder. I grabbed her most unceremoniously and gave her a rare hug.

"You do not have to defend yourself, Euphemia – the house looks spotless, and the children look well fed. Considering we have been away now for nearly five months, I am extremely impressed. Besides, when you hear our story, you will understand why we had been held up."

I sat down to listen to Father's story, looking about at the children's faces glued to every word he said. Hannah was propped up on his knee and Maggie to his left. I thought to myself: *this is what our family does best, storytelling.*

" … and by now we had 261 ton of coal on board. But on the 30th a gale came up from the south with such force the vessel was hove to for twenty-four hours. The monstrous sea was so wild we could not keep her on course, and we were blown out away from New Zealand at a great rate.

On the 31st, the weather moderated a little and we were again able to bring the ship on course. The next day, another gale came up and blew this time with hurricane force. Again, the vessel was hove to for three days and the men were exhausted. As the weather and seas calmed down, we set her on course only to discover her rudder had been carried away and we could not come about. We rigged up a temporary rudder with ropes and hawsers, which was of little use. Day after day we tried to come back on course. By the 4th, we were now more than 500 miles out in the ocean and praying for a miracle. Miraculously, she came to and, being on the wind, sailed by herself to within seventy miles of Wellington. Then the wind came up from the east and we tried desperately to bring her onto a starboard tack. The wind increased to a heavy gale, and we thought we would be lost as waves broke over her freely. When the seas were breaking over the ship, we used a magic trick and put oil liberally on the waters and it calmed the sea.

"Father, how does that work?"

"Well, I am not sure, but my father used it and his before him."

Barbara, the school teacher, spoke up. "It reduces the surface tension of the wave so it cannot form."

"Barbara, is it really true?"

"Yes, Hannah. If you are ever in a storm with Father, you will see how it works. Just a little oil and you will not believe your eyes. It just becomes calm."

"What is surface tension, Barbara?" said Ken.

"See this drop of water? If I let it drop onto this plate, it sits up slightly raised and does not flatten. That is surface tension."

"Well it worked, and on the 10th the weather fined up and we were able to secure a temporary rudder made of ropes. This proved a great success and finally we sighted Cape Farewell on the tip of the South Island. On Wednesday we could see the Cook Strait and then at 8 o"clock finally Cape Terawhiti. A steamer towed us into harbour, and we were saved. We fitted a new rudder and then sailed up the coast here to Auckland."

Hannah had a mischievous look and then said, "Emmie slapped a lady in church today!"

"Hannah, you little rascal! I am sure Father does not want to know about that tonight."

The room was suddenly quiet, and everyone looked at me, except Bess. "It was wrong of me, but I am not prepared to talk about it tonight. Father and Barbara, when the children have gone to bed, I will fill you in on a few things."

"Father, are you getting re-married?"

"Ken, where did you hear that?" I was horrified.

"A girl in my class said it was in the newspaper … your father has married a woman from Australia!"

I looked at Father's face. He hung his head like a little boy. Then he sat up in his chair and rubbed his forehead. Part of me wanted him to feel the pain of shame we had not even begun to feel yet, but I wanted desperately to save him from any more anguish.

"Is anyone hungry? Come on, Maggie. Help me rustle up a few sandwiches. Ken and Dug, can you please go and bring in some eggs, and feed the chooks while you are there. Let us have egg sandwiches. Murdoch, can you cut the bread." Barbara stood up for a second, almost stunned at our efficiency and then slowly sat again with a slight smirk on her face. I put on a pot of water for the eggs and filled the big kettle.

"Murdoch, thank you. Could you go and kill one of the chickens … the hen that has not been laying. I have put water on for plucking. I think Maggie can help you pluck."

I went into the lounge and again asked Maggie to help. "Maggie, can you please put on an old frock and help your brother pluck the chicken." Barbara stood and took Hannah's hand.

"Come, Hannah. We can help butter the bread."

I stared out the window. How could I feel so much anger toward Father when I thought I had lost him altogether? He rose and stood beside me.

"I think you have done well to manage the house the way you have. The children look well. I am sorry about the news report – I really hoped I would be home to tell you all of my folly in person before the news broke. Have you got a copy of the report?"

"Yes. It is in my room. I feel too many emotions to discuss it now, but one of them is anger toward you. Why did you not tell us about this woman!"

"Euphemia, it all happened so quickly. It has been five years since your mother passed and I never thought I would fall in love again. I had feelings stirring in me. I never imagined feeling again for another woman. You have not fallen in love yet; it makes you almost crazy to want to be with that person."

"How do you know whether I am in love or not? I will go and get the article." I stomped off to my room and fished the article hidden in my drawer.

I sat on the edge of my bed, trying desperately to gather my thoughts and calm down a little. For the children's sake, I would not make a scene. I went back slightly more composed. "Here it is, Father. It was published here on the 6th of

September, two weeks ago.”

“Can I help, Phee?”

“Thank you, Barbara. I was hoping you could relax for a few days. You must be exhausted after your ordeal!”

“Phee, I have missed being in our home, and with you all. The sailors are kind to me, but they are smelly, unshaven, rough burly men. I will head away with Father soon again, but for now let me help. We can work together. What is your plan?”

“I would like that. Well I thought it is one-thirty now … if we can get the chook in the oven soon, we can prepare vegetables for the roast now, then while it is cooking we will have time to talk.”

“Give me twenty minutes and I will get changed, unpack my trunk and come back to help.”

“Father, can you please help Barbara with her trunk!”

I set about peeling onions and potatoes. I went to the garden and picked the first small carrots I had planted in early autumn and fetched a pumpkin from the cellar. I quickly gathered all the ingredients and stuffed the chook before sliding it into the oven. Barbara came just as I was finishing off. She now looked quite tired.

“I am sorry, Euphemia; it took a little longer than I expected.”

“How are you, really?”

“Oh, I get exhausted quickly and must lie down for an hour. I sleep like a baby on the ship, it takes me back to being a little girl with Father at sea. It is in our blood, a love of the sea. The fresh air has been wonderful and I sometimes stand with my eyes closed, feeling the wind blow and listening to that magnificent sound of the flap of sails and the creak of the ship as she labours in the mighty winds.”

"How do you think Father is?

"I have never seen him so broken. He does not know it, but I put my head out a couple of times in those terrible storms. He was lashed to the helm shouting at God. "Why? Why? Have I not suffered enough!" and another time he was sobbing as the rain lashed his very soul. I have never seen him so happy to be home with you all.

"Phee, how are you? I sense something different about you. Like you have come alive or something. What is this business with Mrs Shaw in church?"

"Mrs Shaw! Aarhh! It does not deserve our breath.

"But I have secretly been going for history lessons from Uncle John McCallum. I have attended a few WCTU meetings and we won the right to vote only a week ago. I met a young man who was staying at Ruby's for a football game on Saturday. I suppose it has given me a purpose and a hope. Perhaps that is why I am angry with father. He has destroyed some of the things I have hoped for."

"Slow down. Slow down! My! You have been busy." Barbara pulled out a chair and sat down.

"Who is this young man? How old is he?"

"He is handsome. I think he is twenty but he started work at an early age, so is more mature than you would expect. Unfortunately, he is from Wellington, so I do not know when I will see him again. He dropped me off today after church."

"Well you certainly have had a few happenings. What about this upset at church?"

"Stupid woman! The message today was about not judging lest ye be judged. I really felt like the minister was speaking to us about Father. I felt overwhelmed, then when I got to the bathroom those two old gossips were saying that Father deserved to be made bankrupt because he has shamed the good name of folk in the church. I could not bear another minute.

"I am never going back there. You should have seen the looks from the congregation. Uncle John McQuarrie would not even look at me!"

"I know, Phee. Uncle John has not been happy for a while, Father will deal with him."

"Barb, we might just have to go to another church."

"Did you say we finally won the right to vote! That is such great news! At last, we might be seen as having an equal voice. Imagine how many times over the years I have had the humiliation of being asked to bring my husband down to sign for a cheque. I know only too well about having hopes and dreams dashed, Phee, giving up my career."

"Barbara, I am so sorry; I was not thinking."

"No matter. What was that about history lessons? At the office...?"

While we talked about the children and her shopping trip in Melbourne, I had stoked the fire with a few small blocks. The house filled with the mouth-watering scent of roast chicken.

Father came over. "How is the meal coming along? I am hungry tonight; I have looked forward to a roast meal. Phee, I will speak to the children over dinner about Mrs Vine. I will go and unpack my trunk and then come down for dinner."

"Father, can you trim those terrible whiskers. No one will recognise you on the street!"

"That could be a good thing, for the first time ever."

"I have just remembered there is a letter that came the day after you left – it has a wax seal on the back." I rose and took it from the drawer it was hidden in. He held his whiskers as he read it, looking serious.

"Ah, I was expecting something like this. They cannot get blood out of a stone; I can only work the hours God gives me."

I stared at him in silence, not quite knowing what to say. Hannah danced about setting the table while we all pitched in to serve the roast hot.

The sun was just dropping over the hills of Devonport as father came and took his seat at the head of the table. "Father, could you please carve the chicken?"

I lit the candles and put out the linen serviettes. Barbara was just finishing the gravy and pouring it into the gravy boat. "Come on, children!" I shouted. "Dinner is served!"

We all sat, and Father stared silently around the table as he took the hands of those on either side, bowed his head and poured out his thanks to God. We talked about many things but finally Father wiped his mouth and beard and put down his serviette.

"Thank you, everyone, for your fine effort to prepare a beautiful meal. I cannot tell you what a pleasure it is to be with you all again."

"Ken, I would like to answer the question you asked me earlier. No, you are not going to have another mother. However, I did have desires for a woman in Australia. I was staying in Melbourne for two months to make arrangements for repairs to the *Presto*. Perhaps, at a point in my life where many things were not going well, she seemed like a little bit of sunlight in the gloom, and I thought I had found someone quite like your mother – smart, intelligent, witty, and beautiful. That turned out not to be the case: she was instead what we call a swindler, a fraudster. She has taken me to court, and we have been fined £100. On top of our other bills for the repairs to the *Frank Guy* and the *Presto*, we are in financial difficulty and may have to sell this house."

Chapter 24

Confessions and Mrs Vine

"I know this is a great deal to process all at once. I am doing everything I can to repay our debts. I will be away again soon, and Euphemia will continue to run the house."

The children's faces looked suddenly blank. Maggie spoke first.

"What was the ladies name, and how did you meet?"

"Her name was Mrs Vine. We met on a ship travelling from Sydney to Melbourne in May last year."

"Where will we live?"

"Maisy, we will have to rent a house somewhere. I do not know at this stage."

Barbara got up from the table and went out momentarily, returning with armloads of gifts for everyone.

"I know it is not Christmas yet, but I said to Barbara that we need something cheerful tonight with all our troubles."

"Oh, thank you, Father!"

Maggie jumped up, kissing Father and then Barbara too. Hannah climbed on Father's lap.

"My, you are getting big, wee Maisy."

There were many shaped boxes. Footy boots for the boys, dresses for the girls. We all went away and dressed up in our new clothes. It was almost like a party. Maggie went and carried in the new floor rug that Mother had started and we'd finished and, although it was for Hannah's floor, Father was speechless. He looked around at each one of us and I heard him whisper, "Annie, your still here in us."

Hannah jumped off Father's lap and sat on the rug, rubbing her hands across it in delight.

"This is beautiful. I love all the pretty colours! Is this a piece of the green dress I used to have?"

"Yes, Maisy. It is all pieces cut out from old clothes – see, that is a piece of Mother's pale blue blouse."

Next morning, Barbara helped me get the children off to school, then we sat having a cup of tea together. Father dropped in and out, preparing for his next sailing away. He had spoken to me in the morning, wanting to know all the details about the altercation at church. He looked determined to do something.

"Coo wee!"

Eileen popped her head around the patio door.

"Come in, Eileen. How lovely to see you. Please come and have a cup of tea."

"Thank you, Barbara. I will stop for just a few minutes."

Barbara went to the lounge and came back with a present for Eileen. "It is just a little something to say thank you for watching out for the children."

"It was no trouble: they were all so well behaved. What a lovely umbrella. I have always wanted one. The times I walk to the corner shop and get wet with a sudden burst of rain.

Father came through and said he was going out to see Uncle John McQuarrie and Aunt Sarah. "Barbara, did you know that the bill was passed in parliament for women to vote!"

"Really! I am shocked and delighted. I think it is time

women got a little more recognition.”

“Good for you, Barb. I really thought you would be more conservative in your views! What about you, Eileen?

“I am not sure. I have heard a little from a few women and it seems like we are going against the very fabric of what our society was built on. Good family values!”

“I see what you are saying, Eileen, and we have disagreed already in the last few weeks, but we are not casting out our family values any more than men are coming home to do the cooking. We want to have the *right* to be equal and independent.”

“Phee, I agree. Why do you think I became a teacher? There are such limitations on girls’ career options – you can be a nurse, teacher or housewife. As a teacher, I could become a headmistress if I worked hard. When *are* the elections?”

“They are a few weeks from now … on the 28th of November.”

“I hope Father is still here. Otherwise, I will miss out. On the other hand, if we leave soon, we can hopefully be back for Christmas in ten weeks.”

“I will leave you two to have time together. I just called in to see if you needed any help today.”

“Oh, thank you so much, Eileen. It is a rare thing to have time to catch up with my sister.”

“Lovely. Barbara, enjoy your stay and thanks again for the umbrella.”

She swept out the door and we were left alone. I had always been so much younger than Barbara. She had been a mother-figure, but since her return, something had changed. It was like having an older sister for the first time.

“Barb, you were saying before about giving up your career

… how did you feel when Father asked you to give up your teaching to look after Mary and Mother?"

"Phee, it was one of the hardest things I have ever done! I *love* teaching and had wanted to be a teacher since I was a little girl. I wanted to have independence."

"Oh, me too! What a huge sacrifice for you!"

"Well, I got to have all that time with Mother and Mary before they passed away. Now, did I just see Maggie duck into Mary's room?"

"Did you not see Mary's room? Come and see. I had discussed it with Aunty Christine, and she said it was a fine idea." Her face widened in horror.

"What have you done!"

I opened the door and instead of fusty smells from five years of being closed up, it was bright and airy. "Maggie transformed it, scrubbing the floors, new curtains from Aunt Christine and the old sideboard in the basement cleaned up, with the extra curtain she used as a cloth on the sideboard, crocheting the edges.

"Phee, it looks wonderful! And she has quilted the headboard with leftover curtain scraps and buttons off an old coat. I love the picture that Mary painted. Isn't that the fabric from her old dress?"

"Yes, she made a cushion out of the fabric as a reminder."

"Has Father seen it yet?"

"No, I haven't had a chance to show him. Do you think he will be angry?"

"No. Not since I heard the glowing report about Maggie's class. How did you go with Mrs Laird?"

"I enjoyed it, and the children were attentive. She has asked me to come and take another lesson." I looked at her, trying to predict her reaction to my next piece of conversation. "So … I have been going to see Uncle John McCallum at the shipyard to get lessons on our history of shipping. He has been going over much of the business in the hope Father will allow me to be trained to take over, but will there be anything to manage?"

"Phee! I think this is brilliant! Get all the lessons you can. Uncle John McCallum is a great teacher. If you step into that role, you will be prepared, and if not, when you set up your own business one day, you will be ready. What did Murdoch say?"

"I haven't told him yet. I thought I would wait to see what Father said.

"Surely, Barbara, if we have to sell the house and the *Presto* is already gone, it is only a matter of time …" I stopped. Our whole world was about to be turned upside down. "Do you think we will have to sell the house?"

"I am so sorry, Phee. With this extra £100, we have no hope of making it through without selling. This house is only worth about £400 and with *Frank Guy's* repairs …"

"But this is where all of us have been born, and many died. How can we possibly leave these memories? I hate Madame Vine even more now. I do not know what I would do if I saw her in the street!"

"I did see her! In Melbourne. Father had gone into the lawyer's office to present his defence for the trial, and she must have found out we were in town. She came to the Royal Hotel and made an awful scene, calling out in the dining room that he had run away from a marriage proposal and was now trying to seduce another young woman. Which people thought was me, of course. We stood up and fled when she had turned away, leaving half our meal, but she followed us down the street, shouting abuse and making a terrible scene. Many people in their houses opened windows and came out onto the street to see. We had to eat at another hotel for the following days we were there."

"What was she like?"

"Over-dressed, falling out of her top, worn-out shoes and a mouth that would boil an egg. She was pretty and yes, not that much older than me."

"Do you think we will see her again?"

"I am not sure, but this woman will stoop to any lengths to make money."

"Barbara, I have felt angry with Father for bringing shame on our family. The reason I was so angry with Mrs Shaw was that she was right about Father bringing shame on everyone's good name! How does it make you feel?"

"I think sometimes we can hold people up in too high esteem. I have seen Father's insecurities; of late he has felt old, hopeless, and broken-hearted. This woman made him feel like a champion, hope-filled, victorious, powerful and loved again. We all want that, don't we?"

"I suppose one day I will be old and understand. But while I am still young … I am thinking of joining the tennis club or croquet. The speaker last week at WTCU encouraged us to start acting like we are equal."

"Well done you! You could get Murdoch to go with you, then it would seem a little more subtle."

Chapter 25

Catch Up Before They Leave Again

We spent hours over the next few days catching up. Father came back from Uncle John McQuarrie's so upset he said he would never talk to him again. John wished he had stayed in Scotland and not come to New Zealand on Father's recommendation.

"John does not want Aunt Sarah to work in the office anymore! I kept her on even when I could not afford to pay her because she is my sister-in-law."

"Father, I am so sorry. I do love Aunt Sarah! We spoke a few times while you were away. I have been going to see Uncle John McCallum in the office while you were away to learn some of the business. I was hoping that in time you would allow me to manage the shipping here at home for you?"

Father took off his hat and rubbed his forehead. "I had hoped that Murdoch could take over the *Frank Guy*, but I had not thought of you managing everything here in the office. That lad is a born sailor like his Da! What a splendid idea."

"Does this leave an opportunity for me to step in, Father?"

"Yes, if you can persuade Aunt Sarah to train you for a week or two. I know you will pick it up quickly; you are a fast learner and Barbara knows a friend who is fantastic at mathematics and who could keep the bookwork in order."

"Oh, thank you, Father! This is more than I dreamed of!" I wrapped my arms around him.

"It is not going to be easy, Phem, but if you get Eileen to cover a little more of the household chores, we may be able to hold off the vultures. I will speak to John in the office and ask him to help a little till you settle in."

"I am sorry, Father, for upsetting Mrs Shaw. I will go and take flowers and apologise."

"Yes, that would be the right thing to do, but we will not go back there. John is so mad – he does not want to see me again."

"Why does he feel so strongly?"

"He says if I am truly a Christian, I would not have had so many losses. 'Surely God is judging you for all the sins in your life!' he said. I do not know of that; Phem, we all suffer so many times in life, but it is not God punishing us. The good book says, *the rain falls on the just and the unjust alike!'* All I can say is, God has saved me time and time again. I have cried out to him and he has heard my cry. Even in this terrible business, he sent Mr McKenzie to me at just the right moment to warn me of Madame Vine!"

"I went to see Captain McKenzie. He shed a little light on the newspaper article."

"He has been a good friend and brother. It will be sad not to fellowship with him."

"Where will we and the children go to church?"

"I think we will start attending St Stephens Church down the hill instead of Knox. I suppose the children can still attend youth down at Knox if they wish – all their friends are there."

"But these are all the folk I have known my whole my life!"

"I am sorry, lass, but if we sell the house, we may attend another church elsewhere anyway. Phem, this all would have been easier if I had spoken to you before I left. I tried on a number of occasions to tell you, but I felt so ashamed. Please forgive me!"

"Father, I love you. For an old sailor you are a softy: do not marry anyone again without telling us!" We both hugged then he held my face in his crusty hands and looked at me intently.

"You're a bonnie lass! Now, I almost forgot to ask how the class went?"

"It went well, and Mrs Laird has asked me to come and speak again."

"See, lassie, I told you! Well done."

"Father, have you seen Mary's room? Please do not be angry. Come." I held one of Father's huge fingers and led him down the hall; opened Mary's door. He stood in silence looking about and taking it all in, then taking my hand looked at me and said,

"Phee, you may not look like your mother, but you have her spirit. It was long overdue, and I can see you have kept a few of Mary's things. It is beautiful and, with Maggie coming up seventeen, she deserves her own space at least till we move."

"Where do you think we will move to, Father?"

"Somewhere we can afford on a small income."

"I have heard rumours during the election speeches that the government may bring in an old-age pension. You could be eligible, now that you are closer to seventy."

"Hopefully, that is a last resort! That letter was from my partner in the *Frank Guy*, Mr Reid, saying they must start proceedings to take over my share of her, if I cannot come up with £600. Do you know, lass, I have had plenty of conversations with our Father while I have been strapped to the helm late at night. I hold such hope for our success … can this be all that my life is going to amount to? However, I have come back to that truth, 'we are not promised another day'.

How many times could I have fallen like Captain Duncan and smashed both legs or been drowned in the night. At the end of it all, lass, we only have today and each other. These are the most precious gifts of all."

I dug my head into Father's chest and listened to his strong beating heart; we just stood there together for what seemed an age.

"Now tell me, I heard from Maggie, you may have met a friend of Ruby's. A sportsman?"

"Father! We only saw each other a few times and he is back in Wellington. He said you both met years ago when you were extending the *Gailoch* for those nine weeks you were in the harbour of Wellington."

"Well I'll be. Yes, I spoke to a charismatic young man of about eighteen. He was on the opposing team, but I was most interested in the conversation we were having. Perhaps we will meet again if it is meant to be. Well, my dear, I must keep going. We will be heading out in a few days and I have still many customers' goods to organise aboard."

He headed off down the hall, glancing over his shoulder with a smile.

I was daydreaming, wondering if Father would be back for Christmas. Within days they would be off again. I had taken the opportunity to write to Harry twice while Barbara was home, before she went again and I was too busy. I wondered if I would get a return letter at all, knowing that men are not gifted in communication. I would just wait in hope.

While Maggie sat reading a book in the candlelight, she looked up from her book and randomly said, "Who is Frank Lawry? I keep hearing people speak about him."

"He is one of two candidates running in the elections for Parnell. He got voted in last election. He is running against Mr Allen."

"The only things I know of politics are the views our family holds."

"I am the same, Maggie. I had attended a meeting in October in the Parnell Hall to hear Mr Lawry speak. There were thirty ladies present – or, as they called us, the "fairer sex" – listening with great interest. Whenever he finished a point of interest, the whole room applauded loudly."

"There seems to be a real buzz in the air with the elections coming up. What did he speak about?"

"He spoke of things I am not interested in, like property tax and the imposition of a tax on unimproved land and incomes, the East and West coast railway. But he did speak at length about the Female Franchise question.

"He said he had no doubt whatever that the ladies would exercise their judgement with as nice a discrimination as any male elector."

"Do they think that women are going to run down the streets in a mob, beating men with sticks!"

We laughed heartily at the thought of it.

"He went on to say that he had voted against the Bill in 1886, but changed his tune this time when he saw the vote was inevitable to pass the female suffrage. The best bit he said was that, if a woman sat in the Education Board or on the Borough Council, she was perfectly capable of taking her seat in the House of Representatives. She was entitled to that privilege.

"You mean a woman could get into Parliament?"

"Yes! *You* could get into Parliament and one day become Prime Minister.

"He also said, it was predicted that anarchy and mob rule would prevail over the Liquor Act, that some Temperance bigots would nearly like to string up the publicans and have prohibition. Consequently, if that happens, the credits of the colony would be destroyed in the markets of the world."

"I read in one paper they were reporting there will be fights in the polling booths and riots on the streets.

"How ridiculous! But it is interesting that nearly every woman I have met says they are going to vote. I am definitely going to make my vote count.

"How do you best make it count?"

"I have been asking 'who is the best candidate between Mr Lawry and Mr Allen?' On the one hand, the Liberals tried unsuccessfully to stop the Bill by voting it out. So on principle I feel I should vote for Mr Allen in the opposition party. But everyone says Mr Lawry has done a good job over the last six years representing Parnell."

"I think I know what Barbara would say: it is better to choose someone you already trust."

"Maggie, it is even more interesting as there is a tussle going on between Sir George Grey, the past governor of New Zealand, and Mr Lawry fighting to represent the same electorate even though they are both Liberal. Grey has come from serving Newton."

"Is it not odd to have an old governor as a local member of parliament? What will happen, Phee?"

"I imagine Sir George Grey will have to go to another electorate."

"The question is, do you want Richard Seddon in again? I wonder what the outcome will be?"

"I would imagine no one has any idea how it is going to go

with possibly up to 107,000 women eligible to vote. We could all decide to vote in one direction and swing the whole political scene."

"But that is exactly what they think women will do! They are scared woman will vote for prohibition to stop their husbands coming home drunk. We will just have to wait and see … Oh, I showed Barbara your room before she left. She was quite impressed with your resourcefulness."

"Yes, she came and sat on my bed and talked for a while."

"I think I am ready for bed. The fire has died, and the candles are almost spent. It is funny not having you sleeping beside me anymore, Maggie."

"Would you like me to come and keep you company tonight?"

Maggie took her book, snuffed out the main candle and carried the single toward our room. "Actually, after the last few days, it will be nice alone."

"When will you come to our class again. Some of the girls have been asking?"

"I will call past the school and speak to Mrs Laird in the next few days."

"I have been waiting to hear how you got on with Harry."

"What do you mean, Maggie?"

"He is handsome! Ruby said he is twenty years old."

"And you are only sixteen."

"Nearly seventeen. I could tell that you like him."

We both walked off, laughing nervously. I was dubious, but thought Maggie might also have a schoolgirl crush on Harry. I had seen the way she had looked at him on the veranda that day. And he was four years younger than I.

"Good night, Precious. Sleep well."

Chapter 26

House For Sale

The next day I went to check for mail again and there was a letter with the postmark, WELLINGTON. It smelt of sweet perfume. I put it in my apron pocket and, skipped like a schoolgirl home, pulling it out along the way to smell it. I decided to make tea first, to make the excitement last a little longer, but it was almost more than I could bear, the kettle seeming to take an age to boil. I jumped up and wound the grammar phone player, selected a classical piece to listen to, and carefully placing the needle. Then I sat on the veranda with my tea and a piece of Eileen's egg-and-butter cake and carefully teased the envelope open. Out slipped three pages, as well as dry rose petals, which fell onto the deck.

"Good day. Anyone home?"

A tall, handsome man carrying a small leather bag came around the corner as I bent to pick up petals. "I am looking for Miss Euphemia McQuarrie. I am James Frater from W. Frater & Son."

"I am she. How can I help you?"

"Captain McQuarrie asked me to look in on you while he was away, to appraise the house. He said not to list it for sale but to look it over, and if I had anyone looking for this sort of location in the next few months, we could possibly arrange to show them through."

"I am surprised because Father did not speak to me before he left about this matter."

"I happened to be at the port when he was preparing to sail, and we spoke briefly then. Would it be alright to have a quick look through or I could come back another day when it is more convenient?"

"I have not tidied up, but I can show you through."

"I love the view from here, the harbour seems close being above the cliffs like this."

"The house has eight rooms – four bedrooms, lounge, sitting room, kitchen, pantry and scullery, and the veranda. Come, I will show you through the bedrooms at the back first."

We wandered through the house commenting on various things: wood panelling, ceiling roses from Melbourne, a chandelier, and special wallpapers from Sydney.

"You also have the house on a double site, which gives you a little more room. I see you have a plum, lemon and an apple tree. I also love the hedges on the boundary."

"Thank you. What is the demand at the moment?"

"In this area and with these views, this house will not be hard to sell at all."

"Where were you hoping to go?"

"Oh, we had not decided yet. Well, there is nothing that can really be done till Father returns, but if you have someone interested, I can do my best to arrange for you to come through."

"That would be wonderful. I will be on my way. Thank you for obliging me. Good day, Miss McQuarrie.

After I saw him out to the gate, I was not the least bit interested in my cold tea; I was now desperate to get back to my letter, before another interruption.

Dearest Euphemia, thank you for your letters, I was most thrilled to receive them. I agree with your comment that it felt like we had known each other for years. I have also daydreamed about our short time together and look forward somehow to a time when we can be again. I am sorry to hear that your father was swept out 500 miles, that would have been extremely taxing even for him. I am sorry I did not get to meet him again, I must have just missed him.

I had no idea you could use oil to calm the sea.

I suppose he is gone again by now, but it was fortuitous that you were able to speak to him about his trouble with the Lady.

How did you go asking your father about working in the office?

I am sure you are excited about the elections which will be soon after you receive my letter. I don't know what James will do if they bring in Prohibition with all this Temperance movement talk. The men at the pub have a great deal to say about it and are already working out ways to make whiskey illegally. Let me know who you vote for and how your class goes? Try your best not to vote us into a dry colony with all your girlfriends, I do hope they were delighted with your new dress? I look forward to seeing you in it.

Yes, Wellington is crawling with all the dignitaries in town for the elections. We have been extremely busy working into the night. It is upsetting to see so many swaggies living off the streets in these desperate times. We do our best to help out with an odd loaf of bread, but the soup kitchens are full with all the men out of work. Many have headed away to the goldfields just to make any living at all. I have heard many stories from some the Karangahake lads of great wealth in the goldfields and feel drawn to try my hand.

We played a game against them last week and we lost by one point.

John said to remember him to Ruby. My candle is about to die so I will say good night, yours sincerely Harry x

I held the letter to my chest and read it and re-read it. *Oh, this feeling … it is wonderful and painful all at once. When will I see him again?* I decided to go and see Mrs Laird, so I hung out the washing in between another shower of rain and put on my walking shoes. I caught her in her lunch hour, and she came out to meet me in the office.

"Euphemia, thank you for coming to see me. I was going to call into you myself. I have been thinking about you coming to speak, and I think I might get Mr Nicol from his shipyard to come and speak. I am sorry for the preparations you have already made."

"But Maggie said the girls in the class had enjoyed my visit and were looking forward to me returning."

"Yes, well, it is a little awkward, but I am sorry — some of the parents do not want your father's reputation to blemish their young minds in any way."

I was speechless. I had not prepared myself for this at all. "But surely you cannot believe these lies printed of my father. Look at his record."

"I am sorry, Miss, but your behaviour at church last week has not gone unnoticed either. Young minds are so impressionable. I know you will understand. I really must get on. Thanks again. Good day, Miss McQuarrie."

I almost stumbled down the stairs in disbelief. How could people be so fickle!

I called in to see Ruby. We had decided to go to polling day together.

"But, Phee, you have done all that preparation for the class. It is outrageous to just dismiss you like that."

"I will not let her take away my joy of being in that class. Let us forget that and discuss something else. What are you wearing to the polling day?"

"I have a bright red dress and a red umbrella to match my hat and white gloves and shoes. Let us show those dull men what fun it can be to vote! What about you?"

"I cannot wait to show you the new dress Barbara brought back from Melbourne for me."

"Please do tell."

"It is in forget-me-not blue with accordion plaited, wide flowing sleeves, not high on the shoulder like my pink one but full epaulettes of lace. My hat to match has two lovely peacock feathers on the left side, which will match my teal blue broach."

"I cannot wait to see it. Is our plan still to go down early?"

"Yes, we will line up at 8am before Haslett's Hall on Eden Terrace opens at nine."

"Have you heard from Harry?"

"I have the letter here!" I handed it to her, and she read it carefully.

"Phee, I am so excited! He is a fine man." She hugged me. "How lovely of him to send greetings from John." She handed the letter back to me.

"I must get home – I have a pile of ironing that has grown like some monster from the armchair. I will pretend I am arguing with Mrs Vine as I do it."

I arrived home and put my frustrations into cleaning up the house. I filled the iron with red hot coals from the firebox and ironed like a man on a pit saw.

I carefully laid out my festive clothes ready for election day, hoping the weather would stay warm and sunny.

Chapter 27

Election Day

I woke feeling like it was a special day and then remembered: "Election day!" At last! It was wonderful to have something to look forward to.

"Maggie! Maisy! We are going to vote!" I grabbed the bed covers and threw them back.

"It's cold," said Hannah.

"Us!" said Maggie.

"Yes! It is our historical day today, and while you may not be voting, you will remember this day for the rest of your life. The day the first women in the world had an equal right to vote!"

I went straight to the stool in front of my dresser to check my face. Both girls came over, glowing with excitement in the reflection of the mirror. They had laid out their dresses the previous night to prepare for the celebration, and Hannah was already struggling into her heavy linen dress. Maggie, now in her undergarments, jumped up.

"Here, let me help you button that up, Maisy."

"Where will you vote? How will you know what to do?" Hannah said excitedly.

"We will wait down at Haslett's Hall till the doors open and then I am told volunteers and councillors will inform us how to fill out the ballot paper."

Maggie came and helped me with my hair, skilfully tying it up under my hat.

"You are quite beautiful, Phee. And that cream shawl will set off your dress perfectly."

"It does not matter today about beauty, girls. Today we step into a new sphere where we challenge men with equality of the mind."

It was still cool at a quarter to eight as we headed out the door, leaving Bess with the boys. As the three of us waited on the street, suddenly Ruby's carriage came over the hill. She was already calling out.

"You all look stunning! I love your dress – I am quite envious."

She climbed down from the carriage, ran her fingers through the lace and felt the light fabric; she held my hand up and made me spin around, making the pleats flow out like a ballerina. What a delight, and it fits perfectly!"

"Do you think so! Does it not feel divine to be out all dressed up. I am quite excited!"

"Wait till Harry sees you in that!" She grinned cheekily. "And who pray tell are these fair maidens? I have not met your acquaintance."

She took Maggie's and Hannah's hands and did a slight curtsy. They both blushed, looking at one another in surprise.

"You both look so grown up. Are you voting too?" she said, winking at me.

"We cannot vote. We are too little," said Maisy.

"Watch out Parnell, the McQuarrie's are out on the town," Ruby shouted.

Maggie smiled at the thought of it.

James, Ruby's driver, climbed down and helped each of us

up to the seats. "There you are, Miss. How fortunate am I today to have four beautiful women to accompany me to vote!"

James pulled into a grassy verge near the hall and tied the mare to a tree, before bowing to each of us in fun as we alighted from the fine carriage. We could hear footsteps busy on the wooden dance floor inside as we made our way over to the hall.

"Looks like we are the first here."

We took our place proudly outside the wooden four-panel doors.

"This is *so* exciting! Imagine what we are going to tell our grandchildren!" said Ruby.

"Ruby, you will have to marry first."

"Well I am just dreaming ahead."

Maggie and Hannah looked about, trying to recognise people.

"Girls, we will have to wait a little and you will not be allowed in. Just wait for us to vote then we may go to the tea house for cake."

"Come to our place for tea afterwards, Phee? Rewa had a cake in the oven, and the most divine smells were coming from the kitchen when I left."

"Can we, Phee? Can I play with your china dolls?"

"Of course, Hannah. We will take tea in the garden," said Ruby.

It was not long before other ladies joined us and soon there were about thirty ladies lined up outside the double doors. Only a few had a man on their arm. It sounded more like a carnival than a polling station, the air so charged with excited chatter.

"Ruby, look at all the bright dresses and hats. It's like we are all off to a dance."

"And to think they thought there could be unrest."

A few of the young women carried bright umbrellas in case of rain, which they were spinning slightly as they stood.

We were the first through the door when it opened and quietly filled out our ballot papers after being shown what to do. It was the most incredible feeling.

I could not help thinking of Barbara wanting desperately to be part of the vote and thought how excited Mother would be to see all her girls here today. *I am doing this for all women who will step out in courage and unity today!* I thought as I held the ballot for a few seconds before dropping it into the empty box.

I took the girls hands when I exited the hall – it was wonderful to be out together – and, as we strode off, Ruby noticed a serious-looking man in a bowler hat standing outside. He had a black box perched on top of a wooden tripod.

"Phee, what is that?" she said.

The man looked up and smiled. "Good morning, young ladies. I am from the *Auckland Star*. Have you voted this morning?" he said teasingly to Hannah.

Hannah looked at me before turning to him. "We are not old enough to vote, but Emmie says we are pioneers."

"Well, young pioneer, this box you pointed to is the latest in Photo technology. It is a Camera. If you would allow me the privilege of capturing you all, you might have your photo in the newspaper."

"Oh, my, come on, Phee!" Ruby took my arm and grabbed Maggie's hand.

"I came down early with my new camera to capture the first people to vote. How long did you wait?"

"We have been here since 8am waiting," said Maggie. "I think my sister may have been one of the first women to vote."

"Well then, perhaps I could get you to stand over there and stand very still. It is best not to smile as it is harder to hold still for a whole minute."

"How does it work?" said Hannah.

"We take a piece of film and transfer your image through the camera onto a glass plate, then we develop a picture from the negative image in a dark room. That is how a photograph is made. I must say you really do look a pretty picture, most elegant, the four of you. I will get the details of your dresses in a moment, but would you mind just standing here with your umbrella up. Perhaps you girls could sit on that small wall."

"Like this?"

"Yes, that is just perfect. Now, if you could hold perfectly still without moving."

The flash went off, giving Hannah a fright.

"I have a big white dot in my vision from the bright flash!"

"Sorry, Miss. Here is a sweet. It will go away in a few minutes."

He wrote all our details with his fountain pen then thanked us all and bid us Good day. "Thank you, young ladies. You might keep an eye on the papers as there may be a photo of you in the next few days."

We walked slowly along the street and met many folk from the village. Most had sickly smiles and ingenuous greetings. One family took their girls' hands and crossed to the other side to avoid us. Some still spoke to Hannah, who twirled in her dress and danced about with Ruby's umbrella. I tried to keep in mind what Father had said: Life is too short. Make the most of it, but I could not help feeling the quiet flurry building in my heart. Surely Father could not go overnight from being loved and respected in the Auckland community to a pariah? What had he done to them?

Hannah broke into my deep thoughts. "Can we get a toffee apple or some fudge?"

A man had a small table set up and was selling toffee apples and small wrapped packets of fudge in the street. Ruby took a coin out of her purse and bought Maisy and Maggie one each.

"Thank you, Ruby!"

"Be careful with that red toffee; it will stain your dresses. Ruby said, looking concerned.

James found us and escorted us back to the carriage, and apart from the scandal scowls, it had been the most delightful morning.

We had a relaxed morning in the big house, and even Mr Petford was polite about our voting. Maggie sat up straight like a princess and conducted herself in perfect decorum.

Later as we arrived home, Aunt Christine came over with our cousins.

"I will make afternoon tea, and shall we have it on the terrace?"

"That would be delightful. Did you vote? I could not wait to come and hear how you went."

"It was marvellous. We took the girls early and then had morning tea with Ruby. A man took our picture and interviewed us for the paper."

"How exciting! You look so lovely – that must be the latest fashion from Victoria. Who did your hair?"

"Maggie. She's so particular about everything and works with dexterity."

"Phee, she told me about a football player you met? Do tell! It is about time a young man noticed you!"

"Oh, it is nothing. We went to the match and met one of

Ruby's billets. He is younger than me but very much a man of the world. We will see – Wellington is so far away – and I do not even know him."

"What is he like?"

"He has the bluest cheeky eyes and a mischievous smile. He is tall, athletic and very handsome. He's a cabbie to the port and perhaps that's where he has learned to charm the leg off an iron pot." I turned to see Maggie listening in with a glow on her face.

"You do seem very smitten. Did he promise to write?"

"Yes. I have a letter already."

"Phee that is good news. Now I really must get these children home. Children, we are leaving!" she called out. Within minutes they were trundling out the door.

A few mornings later, I was busy peeling vegetables for a pot of soup when Eileen came in with the newspaper. It had the election results, and she had a huge grin on her face.

"What is it, Eileen?

"Just read this!"

"*What*! It is a picture of *us*!! On the front page!"

I read as quickly as I could. Richard Seddon for Liberal had won the election and, once all the votes had been counted, over 90,000 women had voted. This was 80% of the total eligible female population, and only 70% of the men voted, but overall a higher percentage than usual. There were no riots or scuffles but instead it had a festive atmosphere.

> *Three ladies were the first votes to be counted, a Miss Euphemia McQuarrie of Parnell in Auckland, Mrs Emily Gibson and Mrs A.Darcy Hamilton from Taranaki.*

"And might I say, you all look wonderful, even if there is no colour in the dresses."

I looked up at Eileen, and we grabbed one another and danced around in a circle in the lounge while Bess barked.

"How? I don't understand … out of 90,000, mine was the first vote! Can I keep this paper; I cannot wait to show Barbara and the rest of the family. Maggie and Hannah will be so excited!"

"Of course, you can! I will also ask some of the other neighbours if I can have their old papers when they are read."

"I must go and show Ruby! She will not believe it. Thank you, Eileen!"

I threw off my apron and ran down the hill to Ruby's. She had just received a copy from her father and was about to come to me. Mr Petford came past smiling. "You girls are famous now. Surely this picture will draw some attention from some eligible man, then I can marry you off and let some other poor fellow look after you," he said, looking over the top of his spectacles.

"Father, you are most horrid. Come, Phee, let's go to my room."

I could not resist the opportunity to stun Mr Petford's smug face. "We have a little political fame already in our family, sir. Our relative Lachlan McQuarrie, from Mull, was responsible for gathering and uniting Australia as a colony. He was the Governor of New South Wales and was called 'The Father of Australia'."

Mr Petford nervously scratched his head and said, "Well that must be where you get it from, Miss." Then he disappeared back into his room.

"What did he mean by that?"

"Phee, you must admit, you can be direct at times."

Ruby and I sat on each end of her chaise lounge.

"Sometimes people just need a push in the right direction."

Ruby looked out the window. "Did you see the decorations in town today? It is now just over three weeks till Christmas and everyone has already switched out of election mode into Festivities."

"Ruby, I really hope this means folk will forget about our scandal."

"Not this side of Christmas." Ruby smiled sympathetically.

"Well, it has made me busy stocking up the larder with preserves and jams ready to have Father home with us all. As usual, everyone is busy fattening up the Christmas turkey or taking every opportunity to feed their prize Christmas pig. I am not sure what to do about getting a turkey – maybe we will have chicken instead this year."

"Father just buys his off a local farmer. I am sure he could find you one. He says having a pig in the paddock stinks too much."

"Thank you, but something will work out."

"When will the Captain be home?"

"All the shipping reports I have heard so far have said the weather has been fair between Port Melbourne and the Waitemata harbour. If I know Father, he will trim the sails and let the wind bring her home. I really hope he will be home within a week."

"I have spent all week writing Christmas cards and sending

them off. I should have already sent some weeks ago to London. It can be six months to get a reply, and it's May by then."

"I have not even thought of cards. I must get Maggie onto that. Eileen has helped me with my mince pie recipe. I found all the dried fruit in town for my Christmas mince, including apricots, and made it up in a bowl with a good dash of brandy so it can soak for a few weeks.

"That sounds tasty! I have never made them before. We have my older brother and his wife coming to stay, so Rewa is busy sorting out their room."

"Oh, that will be lovely. I know you really miss him."

"I do, but she is Dutch, and I get tired of her correcting nearly everything I say."

"That can be tiresome. I will have the children home from school for the break, and Maggie is finishing up at the end of this year. It will be good to have the extra help at home. I have been working till late getting food ready for the next day. The boys have just had to do more.

"Ruby, do you think it is normal for Maggie to swoon and flirt with Harry?"

"What concerns me, Phee, is I have seen him flirting with her as well."

"Oh, I had thought he was just being charming, and that hers was a schoolgirl fantasy. What should I do?"

"Do not worry about it. She will have someone court her within a few short years. She is a fine-looking lass, it's a wonder she is not courting already. How are things in the office?"

"Uncle John McCallum has been going over how to file our ship logs, how to keep accounts for our inward goods and invoicing our many customers. We have had to get all our books in order for this possible bankruptcy. He wanted me to get all the Christmas cards out to his loyal customers, but there has not been time this year.

"Sarah has helped me for ten days; she was most upset by Uncle John Mac's demanding she finish up and vowed to keep in touch despite what her hot-headed husband says. It is painful to think that I will not be able to freely go to their house until this whole thing dies down, however long that will be." I stood to leave.

"I must go past the baker and pick up two loaves of bread for our soup tonight." I waved out to Rewa and hugged Ruby. "Thank you for the tea."

"I almost forgot … do you still want to go to that Parisian evening? All the girls will be there?"

"Sorry, Ruby. Things are really tight for all of us. Luckily no-one has come to buy the house, but I know Father will put it up for sale as soon as he comes home."

"I can pay for your ticket; it will be fun!"

"Sorry. I feel loved that you would consider doing that, but I must face the reality of our financial situation, as hard as that is for me to do."

Chapter 28

Passions of Delight

Another year had passed almost invisibly. There was a knock on the door, and I looked out to the street and could see Ruby's carriage. I could not help feeling a pang of sadness in my heart over the setting sun of our friendship, as she had not called in months and spoke of other influential friends. Maggie raced to the door as I was trying to remove my apron that had become knotted.

As I came into the hallway, my heart almost stopped. There stood Harry in a new suit, cravat, manicured moustache, and a wide-brimmed tourist hat in brown to match his suit. He had a hint of his tweed waistcoat showing with a fine gold watch chain hanging from the small watch pocket. He held a small gift to one side as he hugged Maggie, who had locked her arms around his neck. He straightened and composed himself as he removed his hat. I thought how fine he looked.

I blushed and my entire body charged with a feeling that filled my heart and legs. I ignored my reticence over Maggie's infatuation, and stood quite stunned.

"What … How … Where have you come from? I did not know you were coming!"

I completely threw myself into his arms. My body lay against his like we had been melded in glass. As I bathed in his strong body, he wrapped his arms around me and lifted me for a second off my feet. My whole body was awash, every pore tingling. I had never felt so overcome with absolute delight. I mustered my composure. "How have you been?"

"Well, thank you! We wanted to surprise you, as I am here again for the annual match. It was Ruby who suggested it."

I hugged Ruby a little awkwardly. "It is certainly a surprise … how long are you here for?"

"We will stay till Monday. I have taken a week off from work and have come straight from the ship to ask if you will join me tomorrow for dinner. I would like for us all to go out."

"Of course, I would love to come. Is John up again?"

"Of course, we are like two musketeers. We are actually working together. I have started a new job since our last letter, working for a livery agent. We are really enjoying it and Mr Lane is certainly an interesting character. It's a long story which I will tell you tomorrow, but I bought a horse, and it won a race last week —made enough for us to come up and take the week off. We have a contract to supply horses to Thames, for all the extra works going on up there in the goldfields."

Maggie was standing back, hanging off every word Harry said.

"How are you, Maggie? You are more lovely each time I see you! The last time I saw you, your hair was in school girl braids."

"You can see I am not a schoolgirl anymore," she said, smiling. "I finished school last year and have been helping manage the house as Phee has spent more time doing office work."

"It looks like you have the place very well organised, like your sisters would. The Captain must be grateful to have your help. This is a nice big house, Euphemia! Do you miss the views of the harbour? It looks like you have extra space."

I glanced at Ruby, hoping she would take the hint. "I miss Eileen and Ruby dropping in, and it is a long way to the shipyards and Queen Street shops from here. Perhaps it is good … there are less highlanders over here in Newton than in Parnell, so not so many folks shun us over the scandal. The English immigrants here do seem to complain about things not being like home."

Ruby stood wringing her hands. "Phee, I am sorry I have not called – life has been hectic."

"I cannot believe it has been a year since the last game; it seems like only six months ago we were all together."

"This year has flown by. We have had all the family up in Martinborough with weddings and celebrations, and soon we will do it again with Christmas."

"Maggie and I have been preparing early this year, squirrelling little things away as we have finances to do it. Father has been working hard all year to try and pay back some of his debtors, but it is one step forward and two back. Every time it looks like he will have a win, there is another repair to do or dock fees to pay."

"What goods is he carrying?"

"Just the same, He has been sailing back and forward to Australia, and Barbara is in a routine of packing and unpacking her bags."

"How is she?"

"Harry," I began to whisper, "she is getting slowly sicker, and I doubt she will go away with Father again. It will be better for her to stay home now and rest."

"At least you will have Maggie to help now. How is the Captain?"

"I am not sure. Even with the sale of the house, it was not enough for him to repay all of his debts. I am expecting him home this week, and the lawyers have said this is it. He has a hearing on the 20th December to decide his fate. No man could have done more."

"I struggle to think that he has slaved away all these years for it to come down to this." His face was genuine as he looked into my eyes. I fought back the tears that had started to well up, but Harry saw it and quickly offered me the little gift.

"This is just a little something I saw and thought you would like."

I carefully unwrapped the paper and the white tissue to find a tiny felt bag. Inside was the most beautiful mother of pearl broach in the shape of a white rose, edged in gold. "Oh, it is lovely!" My face flushed with delight. "How wonderful of you to think of me!"

Maggie carefully picked it up. "Here, let me put it on for you. It looks lovely."

"Thank you so much. You did not have to bring me anything."

"Well, I was thinking of your new dress and thought the broach would go nicely with it. I must get going, Phee. Ruby said her Father needs the buggy. Will we see you tomorrow night?"

"I will be looking forward to it, and will wear my new broach."

"We are going out somewhere nice!" Ruby said, looking over her shoulder as she walked down the hall.

The evening was a huge success. I could not remember the last time I went out in an evening dress. Harry took my hand

and whisked me around the dance floor, tirelessly. It felt like I was floating on air. My body pulsed as I kept looking into his eyes.

We talked together like no one else was in the room, while John and Ruby spent the evening laughing loudly as the drinks flowed. My head spun from the second glass of wine, but I did not tell Harry that I had not really had a drink before, except for a port at Ruby's once. Harry took my hand and escorted me outside into the fresh air. Without a word, he held my face gently in one hand and gently kissed my lips. I held his body close against mine and looked into his eyes. His kisses were charged with magic, and I wondered what it would be like to lay naked with him.

The next few days were a blur. Ruby and I attended the football again, and I tried to get all the time I could with Harry, but my time was limited with this trial coming up, just five days before Christmas.

In the house, we set up Barbara's room upstairs, where there was plenty of fresh air. It was just in time as Father came home on Sunday night, shattered.

Barbara walked in the door, looking pale. Her eyes were sunken slightly and her cheeks were thin. Her breathing was slow and laboured as she came in with her bag. I rushed to welcome her with a kiss.

"Welcome home, my dear sister. I am so glad you are home at last. Can I get you some hot soup and bread?"

"Thank you, Phem. That will be much appreciated."

"Boys, please help Barbara to her room."

I could see clearly it was the right time for her to stay home. We fussed over her to get her settled in. Harry had heard that Father had arrived and came specially to see him as he was leaving for Wellington in the morning. I saw him coming in the front gate, so hastened Father to his room and put on a new shirt and his good waistcoat and trousers.

"Come in, Harry." I met him at the door ahead of Maggie, and held onto his arm like I was never going to see him again. "Come and sit down. Father will be out in a minute. He saw you coming, and wanted to put on something a little smarter, but he is very tired."

We sat close together on the two-seater chair.

"Any excuse to see you before I go., Harry said. "Letters seem to take forever to arrive. It is the happiest part of my day, hoping the postman has a special letter for me. By the way, thank you for your letters. In all the excitement I had forgotten to say."

Just then Father came into the room looking quite smart in a crisp white shirt and woollen, blue trousers. He had already had his hair and beard trimmed for the hearing. He stepped forward, and Harry boldly leapt up and thrust out his hand to embrace in a firm handshake.

"Harry, thank you for dropping by. My daughter has spoken of you a few times," he said, winking, "and I thought it expedient for us to meet."

"Thank you, sir. I just missed you last year when you were delayed coming home and again when you had been in Port Wellington twice from Lyttleton."

"How are things down there, son?"

"Good, sir. My brother James and I are busy doing nights with cabbie work and I am working for a Livery agent. It is like everything is gathering pace with new buildings going up continually. How are things for you, sir?" Harry did not want to be too direct but the intimation in his voice said it all.

"Well we will see. I will do what I can to keep our ship afloat, but at the end of the day I have had a good run and lived a lot of life. It is no one's doing but my own.

"Where are your parents, lad?"

"They are in Timaru and Martinborough. Nearly our whole clan is living up there now."

"Are they not together?"

"No. Father was a blacksmith but got kicked in the head by a horse in '84 when I was five, so he has been in an asylum ever since."

"I am so sorry to hear that. Does he recognise you?"

"No. I have been to visit him a few times, but he does not really know us."

The other children had quietly come into the room. Maggie had put on the kettle and sat down, listening intently, while I arranged the tea service on the table.

"Can I offer you a cup of tea? Maggie has made hot scones. They are one of my favourite things."

"Sir, that would be lovely. We have been living in a small tenement house with a stable beneath, and James' wife is not a great cook."

"What are your aspirations, son?"

"I would like to own a farm one day. There is some nice land they are surveying down south in Kirikiriroa, but it is inaccessible until they put the road through. There is talk of a road one day joining up to Wellington but why would anyone even bother when you can go by ship, It would be weeks journey on a horse."

Murdoch had been listening in, and spoke up. "Father, there is a vehicle that one of the engineers working in the yard spoke to me about. It is made by "Benz" in Germany and powered by some sort of gas engine instead of steam. Apparently, it can carry passengers like a cart. The designer's wife 'Bertha Benz' went 130 miles in it visiting relatives with her two sons a few years ago. This year they plan to build 1200 in a factory in Europe. Imagine, one day we may not need any horses and carts – we could just drive to Wellington to visit you, Harry."

Father laughed. "That'll not happen in our lifetime, lad."

"It is also convenient to stop and feed your horse on the side of the road." Harry winked at Murdoch.

"Father, how do you think it works?"

"I am not sure, Murdoch, but I suppose it must work much like a steam engine."

Maggie came out with a tray and placed it on the table. She carefully poured the tea and offered it to Harry first with a hot scone and jam.

"Maggie, are there any burnt ones?" he said, laughing.

"Beg your pardon?" Maggie said.

"It is alright, Maggie. Last year I burned some scones and Harry kindly took a burnt one from the kitchen to make me feel better." Maggie stood looking at Harry with a mischievous, deadpan face.

"Would you like me to go and burn one for you?"

We all laughed as Maggie continued to serve the tea.

"Thank you, Maggie. This is lovely."

Barbara began coughing in the lounge. I rose and encouraged her to retire to the bedroom, and helped her up the stairs. She looked terrible, having lost so much weight.

"I have been shipping goods through to Thames for the new railway line going into Paeroa which should be opened by next year," Father said. "They are also going to carry the line right through those mountains to Thames. Harry, with your energy, you should look at going there or the goldfields in Kunatunu, as there are still opportunities to make good money there – plenty of people and settlers prospecting. With your skills, you could be managing a work crew."

We talked for nearly an hour after the children went to bed and Father talked about gold and the Scotia fund. It was good to hear them both roaring with laughter as they told stories from the dockyards. I had not expected Father to get on so well with Harry. Finally, he said goodbye to us all, and I walked out onto Gladstone Road with him. He kissed me and then we held each other close for what seemed an age. I wanted to be free to go with him and felt deep sadness as I watched him ride away into the dark night. How long would I have to wait to see him again?

Father sat waiting and rose to his feet as I came back into the room.

"Harry has a good heart and is certainly a clever businessman. He has done well to rise up out of poverty." Then he whispered, "I have a Father's intuition that perhaps Maggie was also flattered by him?"

I whispered back, "Father, I am hoping it is nothing but a silly fantasy, but I will speak to her about it when the time is right. It was wonderful to hear you two men laughing."

"He has already experienced a great deal of life and is most interesting to speak with. I look forward to many more conversations in the future, perhaps. I am off to bed it has been a big day and we must have our wits about us tomorrow."

"Father, do you think *she* will show up in court."

"I am not sure. That woman seems to be capable of anything. Good night, my dear. Thank you for all the work to prepare for this hearing." He kissed me gently on the cheek as he went. "You have become a strong woman."

It was the 20th of December. We had been preparing for the bankruptcy hearing for months. I sat in the quiet, contemplating the journey that had led us to this day. We had survived the *Flying Cloud* horror, the crippling bankruptcy of '88, losing Mother, Mary, wee Annie, little Murdoch and now we were about to lose Barbara. We had suffered through two costly shipwrecks and now, as if wringing out the final three drops from a cloth, Father's passion, livelihood, and dignity were about to be ripped away, like a dog tearing the head off a chicken carcass. This She-Devil might have thought a McQuarrie was an easy target, but she would rue the day she backed Father and I like wild dogs into a corner.

I felt charged with purpose as I quietly laid out my red dress, gloves and hat for the morning. Whatever challenges tomorrow brought we would weather that storm too.

Chapter 29

Lions Face Off

The afternoon was warm as we arrived before the office of the official assignee for Bankruptcy.

"Good morning, Euphemia. it is lovely of you to attend the hearing with your Father."

"Thank you, Mr McGregor. Wild horses would not keep me from facing that Devilish woman."

"She is here. I saw her come in earlier."

"Good. We are ready for a fight! How do *you* feel, Father?"

"I did not sleep well. I feel old, like a lion who is about to be beaten by its younger adversary. I have dreaded this day for too long, but I have faced off against the fiercest storms and prayed 'God I am in your hands now'."

"Hector, we both realise that, for you, standing up to this woman is going to be the hardest storm you may have weathered yet. Your greatest strength is rising up when the sea is crashing over you, and the tempest is drowning you in ocean waves.

"This is that day, but *she* also represents your greatest weakness, *everything* that you hate most – thieves, cheats, and liars.

"Today they will try and make you look like one of them, a cheat and a liar. Do not give in to the bait. I know you – you would go to the gallows and face your accuser like a true

Highlander, eyeball to eyeball, dirk in hand to the death. Today is the day to steady your dirk in its sheath, still your mind as you take the stand. Like the good book says, *"Quick to hear, slow to speak and slow to anger."*

We entered the dark fusty courtroom and took our seats at the front. I sat in a seat behind Father, and as I looked up, there she was.

This fox had stripped the last ounce of dignity from my Father, who would himself have stripped naked if he thought someone needed his clothes. She was dressed like a lady of the night, red blushed cheeks, a pale face with big dark eyes, fancy red hat, and a full-hooped dress in red crepe. I wanted to leap the seats and rip her throat out. Smiling like a fox just before it tears an animal apart, she blew Father a kiss as he glanced her way. The judge acknowledged Father with a nod as he entered the room.

"All please rise for the honourable judge."

Honourable remains to be seen, I thought, *if it's anything like the hearing Father spoke of in 1868.*

"I call this court to order. Please take your seats.

"We are here today to consider council's opinion on the validity of the transfer of the ownership of the defendant's ship, the *Frank Guy*. We have a few creditors here today, laying claim to her and we will hear their arguments presently.

Madame François Vine whispered into the ear of her lawyer at regular intervals – he looked more and more embarrassed as her whispering became louder. A long discussion took place concerning certain transactions in connection with the *Presto* and *Frank Guy*, which became almost heated at times with Mr Reid as he did his best to keep calm.

Father was on the stand and doing his best to keep his head.

"Hector McQuarrie, under oath, what did you do with £250 which you received in Australia for the half share in the wreck of the Presto?"

"I had not received it personally; it was paid directly to Mr John Reid, my partner of the *Frank Guy*."

Mrs Vine's lawyer then stood to ask a question, but *she* was interjecting so much he could not speak. Suddenly she stood and, with her arms out on the table in defiance, asked Father directly, "After I got a judgement against you in Australia, did you not say that you would make a certain sum of money over to someone else so that I would not get it?"

She had leant forward on the table, ready to strike. Obviously, she had not sailed two weeks from Melbourne to go home empty-handed and would use all her limitless theatrical skill to bring to bear her fury.

"No. I did nothing of the sort."

Her whole body erupted in protest, and she shouted from behind the desk. "Yes, you did! You did!! I *know* you did!"

The judge's gavel banged repeatedly on the block as he called for order. "Madame Vine, sit down! I will not have an outburst like that again. You will be removed from the courtroom."

She flung her arms in the air in disgust, flashed disparaging glances at the judge and her lawyer. This was her lead role, acting the wounded widow in a star performance. She gripped her hat, which had come slightly unpinned with her many operatics.

Mr Captain Rugg, who represented one of the creditors, asked Father if he had removed anything from the *Presto* to the *Frank Guy* after the former vessel met with a mishap in Australia?

I could see Father was still furious after the emotional outburst from Madame Vine.

"We saved a boat and some sails which were aboard the *Presto* and took them to the *Frank Guy* in case they went missing."

"Did your partner Mr Reid know of their removal, or did you render any account of it to him."

"No, but I tried to sell her for him in Auckland, unsuccessfully, as I could not secure a buyer. If I had, Mr Reid would have got the money!"

"What became of the boat?"

Father was getting hot under the collar, knowing full well he had done the right thing, and was being accused of lying.

"She was smashed to bits in a hurricane off Kaikoura last year, so if you want it you'll have to go a long way for it!"

There was light-hearted laughter across the courtroom.

Mr Palmer then put a question to Father in reference to a certain sum of money. "You stated you had paid to Captain John McKenzie £231. Were you aware that Captain McKenzie denied having received the money?"

"I knew nothing of the sort!"

At this stage, seeing she was not going to get the £100 owed to her from the Supreme Court hearing in Melbourne, Madame Vine erupted.

Some desultory discussion ensued, with no definite resolution being arrived at. Her lawyer had tried unsuccessfully to restrain her as she cast accusations about from one person to the next while the judge called for order. Finally, the guards took her one on each side and dragged her from the court with her screaming blue murder. It was decided then to adjourn the meeting *sine die (Without day)* so those interested in the *Frank*

Guy might have time to consider the possibility of making a satisfactory arrangement with creditors.

As Father came off the stand, I suddenly saw him older than I had ever seen him. Till that day, he had seemed, to me, like Samson, able to pull down a palace with his bare hands. Now, as I saw him walking toward me, grey bristly beard, slightly balding and limping on one hip. It was as he'd described it: an old lion beaten and bruised, looking for a warm spot under a tree to lick his wounds and rest awhile.

He leaned over to me whispering, "I need a stiff whiskey."

I stared in shock. Father had never had a drink that I knew of.

We spoke for a moment with Mr McGregor before heading out, leaving the dark court room behind. Madame Vine was waiting to pounce as, clutching her bag with white knuckles, she strutted directly toward us, shouting.

"Do you really think I was going to marry *you*, old man! Not under my real name, *fool!* I am going to get you for every penny!"

She spun on her heels, tossed her head and strode away.

I clenched my fists and mustered every ounce of my will not to grab her by the hair and throw her down the stone steps.

The corridor had become hushed as everyone looked our way. I closed my eyes and took a long slow breath, thinking of the added humiliation we could suffer if I did. I turned to Father and said, taking his arm in a firm grip, "Come on, Father, our chariot awaits. Let us leave all thoughts of *her* behind. It is like you said, it is not over yet, and we are not promised tomorrow. We only have today!"

He looked up at me, all the fight gone from his eyes as he stood quietly linked in my arm. I put my shoulders back as we strode out the huge timber doors, holding our heads up as we made our way down the stairs. Many people milled about waiting to interview us for the local news but I politely waved them aside and beckoned to a cabbie.

Father climbed into the buggy with difficulty, and the two horses looked like he probably felt, tired and worn out. Queen Street was bustling with horses and carts as we stepped off the curb and crossed the dirt road. Many tall four-storey buildings had gone up over the last few years, all built on gold and new settlers.

"Can I help you to your seats?" A young girl held Father's chair as he sat down.

"Could we have tea and cake please?"

"Certainly, Miss. I will bring it right away." Father had taken off his hat, and I straightened his comb-over hair that had gone sideways. He loosened his waistcoat a little and looked at his gold watch.

"Barbara bought this for me when she was working as a teacher. It was I who asked her to come and help nurse Mary and Annie. Have I done this?"

"Father, that is a sad thing to say. She told me that it was her privilege to nurse them because she got to know them and care for them right to the end. Look, in five days we have Christmas, and I do not think Barbara will make another one. We must somehow put this behind us to make it a special festive celebration!"

"But, Phem, we have no money to even buy a turkey?"

"Father, Murdoch and Maggie have been working, and I have been doing bookkeeping for Fraser & Tinne. We have squirrelled little things away and do not need expensive gifts, as long as we are together."

The young girl brought out a silver tea set with matching sugar bowl and cups, dark fruit cake and a small container of whipped cream.

Father bowed his head and put his hands over his face in shame, and said, "How did we ever get here, lass? What am I going to do now? *She* has tipped the scales, and my life is over!"

"That Devil will not have a moment of glory in our house while I have breath. You will retire and let us look after *you* for once."

"Every time the wind comes up, lass, I will want to go to sea. The only choice I have is to dig a hole in the garden and put away my compass and sexton where I cannot find them. Since I was a little lad, all I wanted was to build great ships, conquer the deep ocean and harness the wind like taming a wild bull elephant. What have I left? Even all the fine men I have trained and sailed the oceans with will not speak to me after this final humiliation."

"Father, let me tell you something … are you listening?"

He stared at me, his eyes dark and troubled.

"You have lost *so* much, but not everything! You have suffered terribly, but you still have breath. Your heart has been crushed, but you have two arms and seven children who love and adore you.

"We had a father lost at sea, shipbuilding, conquering the ocean. I have spent my life looking out to the horizon, watching patiently for your return.

"We have been waiting, but this is not the end; this could be a new beginning. Curl up under a tree and lick your wounds but come back to us – a new life, with your children, your grandchildren awaits.

"When Mother died, it seemed like we had lost our only

parent, now the children are about to lose Barbara, the only Mother they have!

"And this is another huge sacrifice on your part, but we need you!"

The Captain just stared at me in stunned silence. He picked up his cap and fiddled with it contemplatively. "I have never had you speak to me like this before; you truly are a spirited woman. Every word you have spoken is difficult to hear, but you are right." He took a sip of his tea, deep in thought. Then he straightened his tired back as if strength was pouring back into his heart.

"I have never sailed these shores before; I will need your help to find the reefs and sand bars. And I may have days where I am becalmed and need your grace … as a grumpy old man. But I want this! … I want to be useful and celebrate your lives right now. I love you all so much!"

He took a bite of the cake, rose to his feet, put on his hat and took my hand.

"Phee … into the storm."

Chapter 30

All Together

When we arrived home, there was an envelope standing on my dressing table. I recognised the handwriting immediately. Of all days to get a letter from him, I needed it today. I took it and sat on the back steps in the afternoon light. The most beautiful Christmas card with a letter was inside.

Dearest Euphemia

Merry Christmas! How are you? You are often on my mind. I find myself wondering what you are doing each day. Have you had your Fathers hearing yet, I am hoping for a favourable verdict? Your father is a good man, please give him my sincere regards.

How is Barbara also? I can only imagine it is a big job looking after everyone in the house now with two extra people to care for. I know your preparations for Christmas are well underway; it will be light relief considering the year you have endured.

I moved to Martinborough, as James lost his house. My sister Emma remarried, and has moved up from Timaru and I am living with Mother for a time. Seven out of nine of us children live here now in this growing community. There is good grazing land here, some owned by the Harris family which my brother and sister have married into. Who would ever believe we would end up a family of farmers? I told you Mary married Jack Gaskin last year, well she now has a baby on the way.

James is here cutting flax just to get by after his gambling debts finally caught up with him, but he and his wife are not very happy. He lost the house and stable in Pririe Street as he owed an immense sum of £130, so he headed to Manuwhatu for a stint to get away from his gambling mates but ended up in court there too. As you can imagine, he has been under pressure and got caught yelling obscenities at a customer and fined for obscene language. He was in jail for 14 days with hard labour after not showing for the hearing. They caught him and made him do the time in Timaru. I think it was the last straw for Mother and she gave him a stern talking to. I am not sure I will stay here long. I have been thinking a great deal about the advice your father gave me, to try the goldfields and see what opportunities are there. My brother John is there now and says it is hard work but he has found enough gold to make a good living. He has always been quite the sportsman and is playing in one of the top teams. I hope this finds you all well. Please give my regards to the boys and your sisters too. Yours sincerely Harry Bagust xxx

I did not have time to reply as Maggie and I were preparing

for Christmas day on the morrow. We worked late into the night in the sitting room wrapping presents for the children. Things were tight so we had been creating little gifts over the last few weeks for Santa's stockings. We could not afford a turkey this year, so Aunt Christine found us a goose. We spent hours preparing it and I rose in the dark hours of morning to get the stuffing made and vegetables prepared. The barometer read 72 degrees and it was cloudy, humid and calm. The first rays of sun appeared just for a moment under the clouds on the horizon, before disappearing again. Hannah came through in her nightdress, looking sleepy. I wiped my hands and crouched, sweeping her up and spinning her around.

"Hannah! It's Christmas!"

"I saw the stockings on the mantel in my room. Can I get mine down and see?"

"Yes … bring it out if you like. I must get this bird in the oven and prepare food for lunch. Try not to wake Maggie, she will be tired."

"That is a big dish!"

"It's for roasting the goose. We borrowed it off Aunt Christine."

Hannah ran off very excited.

The little fat lobes spattered away until I had enough for basting the bird, which I rubbed with salt as Aunt Christine instructed. Barbara had helped make cranberry sauce and prepared the steamed pudding yesterday, but she was exhausted after only a short while and slipped away to bed again. I slid the bird into the range, hoping I had not made it too hot for a slow cook.

Hannah's face shone with delight as she came running through with her soft doll.

"Look, it even has a pretty dancing dress!"

"I am so glad you like it. Take it in to Maggie!"

Murdoch came out looking smart.

"Merry Christmas, Murdoch!" I gave him a kiss on the cheek. Look at you all dressed up!"

"This is my new shirt."

"It looks very smart. Go and thank Barbara for finding the fabric in Melbourne."

"It seems strange being off work on a Tuesday. People are saying that Christmas day should become a holiday so everyone will get paid."

"That will probably never happen, but imagine … then families can all be together."

The house was cosy, and the boys came out with their Christmas stockings. A serious competition ensued on the lounge floor over the twin's glass marbles but, there was a quiet content about the house with Father and Barbara home. Father was particularly relaxed, especially on calm days when there was no hope rising in his heart of stealing out to sea.

Hannah had asked to help, so she set the long table with the pretty decorations the children had made. They had caught the festive spirit with a fir branch that Murdoch found for the corner of the room. Buntings strung across the ceilings and little red balls made of wool were fastened about the tree and room. They had cut out and coloured Angels, lanterns, stars and even made a nativity scene.

"Maisy, those decorations look so joyful."

Chocolate fudge and steam puddings were set aside cooling, filling the house with sweet candy aromas. I took the roast in and out of the oven, basting the bird every thirty minutes till it was golden brown and crunchy. Maggie and I worked feverishly in the hot kitchen, at last filling the table with a colourful array of steaming hot food.

"Father, could you come and cut the meat? Murdoch, can you please round up the boys."

A hush descended over the table as we took our seats, gazing at the feast in front of us. As Father prayed, everyone bowed, but I took those few moments looking around at our beautiful family. I looked at Barbara and was suddenly gripped by the realisation that she would not be sitting there next Christmas. She caught my eye and without a word winked in a telling way like she knew what I was thinking.

Chapter 31

Barbara's Passing

Harry had also been on my mind all day, and I wished he were here to celebrate New Year's Eve in a few days. I had dreamt of him holding me, especially over this time of Mother's remembrance! I decided to write to him.

Dear Harry

It must have been a wonderful Christmas celebration with all of your family together in Martinborough. What does it feel like to have your first Christmas all together living in a small community again?

We had one of the nicest Christmas celebrations in years with everyone here. Even the goose I nervously prepared was succulent with only a little burnt piece on one side, which I know you would have enjoyed. I had thought of coming to visit you with Maggie many times, but I do not think I can get away at present. Mother's Remembrance Day went well. It was a special weekend with Aunt Christine and all the family over which Father organised on the 29th of December. We share funny things and fond memories after supper in the lounge. Everyone brought food for dinner and contributed skits, music and recitations, well into the evening. Have you been playing your Accordion at any events? I look forward to hearing you play? I dream of dancing the new year in with you, if only we could be together again? You asked about Barbara. She is suffering severely when she coughs, I know this will be her last New Year's Eve celebration. The Doctor has called often and advised that we put her into a separate room to contain any spread. We boil her sheets, handkerchiefs and clothes regularly and keep her room warm and dry. It is painful to see her slowly fading away and it brings back memories of Mother and Mary. She has little respite from her cough, which keeps her awake at night and leaves her weak and exhausted.

We have taken turns to sit by her bed reading her the latest news from Melbourne, telling funny stories or taking her meals of chicken broth.

The Doctor last week recommended she go into a sanitorium, given the young children in the house. We are against it, but she is afraid one of us will become ill. Father goes and visits her often and reads to her.

Our Highland folk have been so kind, often dropping by with a meal or words of encouragement. Father was most encouraged by this and has a new strength.

The weeks and months passed by without word from Harry but I was delighted when Ruby popped over. I was surprised at how much I talked as we sat having tea and catching up on many things; it had been an age since I had caught up with a friend.

"Ruby, it has been difficult nursing Barbara these past few months seeing her fade away, but it is good to have her home."

"How long do you think she might have?"

"I think Barbara could be in her last days."

"It is a lot of extra burden for you all, but lovely for you all having her here."

"We have been so vigilant to keep things separated and especially with the children. Father is not concerned as he says, 'I will cast my lot in the hands of God – what will be will be.'

"It is so good to see you again. I have missed you a great deal, Phee; we have had so many laughs together."

Oh, I forgot … the doctor often calls around this time. Are you happy to stay? I am expecting him to let us know her condition today. It would be lovely to have your support."

"Yes, I am happy to."

Within half an hour his little cart rolled up outside. It was amazing to have Ruby here at just the right time.

"Good afternoon, Doctor. Thank you again for calling."

He came through with his little bag. "It is the least I can do to help. How is she today?

"It is agonising to hear her breathe and be in so much pain. I am wishing she be released from this world soon."

"This disease is a terrible thing; I have seen too much of it. Well let me see her now." He found his own way up the stairs to her room. I could hear her coughs as she tried desperately to speak.

"She is very sick. I had not realised she had gone downhill so far."

"She can only talk in a whisper and says every cough is like someone has taken a knife and stabbed her lungs. I have heard father sobbing quietly at times in his room at night. He is reliving all the many deaths he has suffered."

The Doctor came back down. "I have given her a little more for the pain. Have you noticed any blood on her handkerchiefs?

"Yes. She sometimes coughs up little shows of blood."

"I am sorry, dear. It will be any day now! Do your best to keep her warm. There is not much else that can be done but to keep her comfortable."

"Thank you, Doctor. I will send one of the children over if we have a sudden change in her condition."

"Very well. Good day, ladies. I will see myself out."

Ruby hugged me as we stood there trying to process the gravity of Barbara's sickness.

"Phee, you will have to let Harry know. He will be concerned for you."

"I have not heard from him in months – I do not understand. Have you had any letters from John?

"No. John has not written lately, but he is not good at communication. I wonder why Harry has not written?"

"I do not know, but I am sure he has a good reason. It is not my concern right now. I will have my hands full preparing for the next few weeks if Barbara's time is near.

"The last I heard of John he was working in Ohinemuri but it does seem strange that he has not written either? Perhaps he is just working long hours. You must let me know how I can help you with any preparations. I will come and make some fruit cakes this week and store them for any guests."

A few days later, there was a tapping on the floor, which was Barbara's best way to call us to her. It was the 9th of July 1895.

I went into Barbara. She was propped up and called for us all. She had completely lost her appetite and begged us not to try and feed her any more. A week passed. She must have known because after she had said goodbye to each one of us, she asked Father to say a prayer over her.

The Doctor waited for us to finish, then made her comfortable. She slipped away peacefully in the night.

I have never known the house to be so quiet. For days we all moved about the house in a daze. I can hardly remember the preparations for the funeral, but it was good to have Father's diligence in preparing all the little details. Barbara was laid in peace alongside her other brothers and sisters in Symonds Street cemetery. She was twenty-seven years old. It was so final as the minister read and we all took turns to sprinkle soil on her coffin. *Goodbye, dear sister, we will live this life for you.*

Chapter 32

Death and Life

All the grief of the last few years seems to come in like a flood. Again, we faced the loss of a second mother and sister. I wished more than ever to speak to Harry and could not understand why he had not written.

Most folks avoided our home like we had the plague, as many in the community treated families who had lost members to tuberculosis – they just didn't want to risk contracting the disease themselves.

If that was not bad enough, Father's final loss came via the newspaper a week later, following an article from January.

> *There was a meeting today of the creditors who resolved to take steps to test the validity of the transfer of the Barq 'Frank Guy' from the Bankrupt to Mr John Reid, as the creditors wound up proceedings.*

A few weeks later, on the 15 August 1895, the debtors accepted John Reid's offer of one shilling in the pound. And I had finally received a letter from Harry.

I was in no mood to receive word from Harry and, although I was curious, my heart was full of anger at his insensitivity.

It is always a nervous moment receiving letters from the postman at any time, as many lately had not brought any joy. I sniffed it gently, but there was no scent. I took a small stick from the hedge next to me and used it to tear open the envelope. I could hardly breathe as I read the words.

Dear Phee,

I am so sorry for not writing all these many months. The longer I delayed, the more I agonised at how I should relate my folly.

Three months ago, I met a young woman at a dance. Her name is Emily Linders. I had been drinking heavily and later in the evening I dropped her home. Unfortunately, one thing led to another and, although we had not seen each other again, she arrived on my door one night saying she was pregnant.

Her father, being of strict German descent, was not happy and urged us be married immediately. I did the honourable thing and asked for her hand in marriage.

"MARRIED!" I shouted.

It was a sad state of affairs for we married in the registry office and then within months she lost the baby. She was in great distress, and I could not console her. I came home to her one evening and she was gone! A note on the table said she would start a new life in Australia.

Her bag was gone, and a few of her things. She said not to track her as she had used a false name

I screwed the letter up and threw it into the garden. "Bastard! How could you!" I could not go back inside; instead, I walked, in shock, my mind filled with questions. Then a tempest of emotions filled my heart. I felt enraged as waves of anger and disbelief flooded my mind. I could not even imagine being with him after him giving himself to another! *What was he thinking? I do not want him back! I hope she returns; it will serve him right!*

I found myself outside the graveyard in Symonds Street and there was Mother's grave. I ran to her plot and threw myself on the still freshly dug ground from Barbara's burial. "I wish you were here! My heart feels like it will break. Is this love?"

I curled up in a ball and just lay there, looking at the bunch of dead flowers of Barbara's, and decided at that moment he was dead to me.

I must have drifted off because I came to and was aware of

someone standing over me. She looked at me and for a moment, I did not recognise the lines on her face.

"Euphemia! What are you doing there?"

"Eileen!" I scrambled to my feet and threw my arms around her, nearly choking her.

"How did you find me!"

"I was visiting my Rosie with fresh flowers, which I do each week and thought I would come by and visit Annie as I passed by. You looked dead on top of their grave."

"Oh, Eileen, I am dead," I said bitterly, "deep in my soul! Harry married another woman! I have lost Mother and Barbara – I am managing the house and trying to earn enough to feed us all – I have the children at school and Father grieving over Barbara, but he is broken. I have never seen him idle. It is like he is completely lost at sea."

We sat down on a park bench and she took my hands.

"I am so sorry I have not been over. I started helping another family with their domestics and it takes up all my available hours in the day.

"Why don't you reduce your burden a little. Send the twins to Aunt Christine's for a few weeks, Hannah has spent time in Whangarei already with her cousins. Ask Hector to go and take her, to stay for a spell. She could go to school up there, and Hector could call on his close friends in Mathesons Bay. Then come and stay with me for a week and leave Maggie to look after the house. Murdoch will be at work so she can have time to herself too."

I looked into her shining face which was full of compassion and kindness, and decided that was what I would do. It took a week to organise but everyone was packed with little gifts under their arms and the children were excited at the thought of having an adventure and a change of scenery.

I settled in with Eileen and enjoyed working alongside her, baking cakes, and when she was out and the house was silent, I dived into a book and quieted my mind, lost myself in another's story. I could not remember the last time I had curled up in a chair in the sunlight and buried myself in a novel.

Then one morning I decided to head home, past the rose gardens and up past Mother's grave again. As I came along Gladstone Road, I saw a horse and cart parked in the yard. *Who can that be! I do not recognise that cart.* I called out as I entered the house.

"Yoo-hoo!" I was feeling thrilled at seeing Maggie as I had not seen her for eight days now, and we had much to share. I could hear the gramophone playing and as I came into the room, there was Harry, dancing with Maggie.

They threw down their hands, and Maggie ran to the gramophone, lifting the needle.

"What?! How *could* you! Is it not enough that you are already *married!* I hate you! I never want to see you again!" I yelled at him.

He tried walking toward me but I backed away.

"I came to see you. I want to be with you!"

"*GET OUT!*"

"Please, Phee. Do not do this!" Harry begged.

"Go, just leave!" I followed him to the front door and threw his hat at him. "Take your hat and your fancy words, and do not darken our door again."

I slammed the door and, leaning back against the wall, slid to the floor. I sat and stared at the floorboards, trying to gather myself. "That sneaky bastard!"

Maggie had run round the back and I could hear her speaking with Harry as he left. I rose to my feet and climbed the stairs slowly to my room and, from the window, watched his cart leave. *Harry, Harry, why?* Part of me wanted to run after him down the street. But instead, I threw myself on the bed. *What do I do now?*

I could hear the stairs creaking quietly as Maggie made her way up. I sat up as she entered the room. She stood in the doorway and we just stared at each other.

"He came to see you! I had not talked to anyone in days; I made tea. I had the music playing for my new song on Sunday with young Hector."

I blankly stared, stunned, and did not know what to say.

"Do you like him?" I said flatly, "You cannot hide it. You have swooned over him since we first met."

"Phee, I really like him! But I know he could never be mine – he is in love with you!"

"He has behaved so badly. I will not have him again. He is closer in age to you."

"What are you saying?"

My heart was being ripped out again, but until that moment I had not thought of myself as the least bit maternal. Was I going to deny my beautiful sister the chance at happiness just because I wanted desperately to be kissed and held in a lover's embrace? *Mother would have chosen to sacrifice her own needs ahead of ours – and this is what I must do now.*

"Maggie, I want you to be happy. If he feels the same way toward you, you have my blessing to pursue a relationship with him."

The voice in my head was loud, like a devil perched on one shoulder. *What am I saying!? I must be mad! Euphemia, this could be your only chance at love! Back down from your pride – he will be yours to have and hold.*

"Do you really mean that!" Maggie pressed, drawing closer as she spoke.

"Come!" I stood up, and we embraced.

"I have seen you together; you seem to get along so well."

"What will Father say?"

"Don't worry, I will speak to him … when the time is right. I must go, I came back to pick up my scarf. I will be home in a few days."

I took my scarf and almost stumbled down the stairs; hugged Maggie at the front door. "Are you alright?" I asked.

"Yes. Are you sure you will not stay for lunch?"

"No, I must clear my head. Where is he staying?"

"At the Imperial," Maggie said, looking helpless.

"Go, find him and take tea, where everyone can see you." I was stern and motherly. "Remember, he is a man of the world; he has already seen much more in life than you. Do not throw yourself at him. Give him a chance to chase you as you play hard to get. I love you!" We hugged again and squeezed each other tight.

I walked down the street, not looking back as tears rolled down my face. Something in my heart died, but for Maggie it would be life.

A Note from the Author

When I was a boy, I had an etched glass picture on my wall, with a background picture of two sailing ships fully rigged in a wild ocean. It was scripted in old text and I would lay there trying to work out what secret message it held in its mediaeval letters. I deciphered it over and over again:

One ship sails East and one ship sails West
by the self-same wind that blows
it's the set of the sails and not the Gales
which determines the way it goes.

It was one of those pictures that nobody knew what to do with, so it hung on my wall. I'm was pretty sure the picture was passed on by my great grandfather, Hector McQuarrie. I would imagine being on one of those ships and wished I had been left an old, worn, brass compass or pirate's gold. Perhaps that was exactly what it was: a message of gold, a secret message for life's compass.

I have written this book in tears at times as I have tried hopelessly to put myself in his shoes, all the time thinking that, if he had set his sails slightly differently, he might have enjoyed a totally different life.

Hector toiled and laboured to succeed, and although he achieved more in his seventy-eight years than most people would ever dream of in one lifetime, the immense losses he suffered at every turn must have left him many times broken.

I have wondered what kept him going? The set of the sails?

My own children have said, "Dad, perhaps you can see something of your own journey in his story." Perhaps this is true and no doubt there is a little of Hector hidden away in my DNA.

Many of our friends and family have said to us over the years, "You are the hardest workers we know!"

Perhaps that is why I have often been confronted by that question, "How much is enough?"

Over the years, with a bit of that same entrepreneur spirit, we have invested in many things. As I get older, I realise that the best things in life are made up of S.O.M – Simple Ordinary Moments.

Did Hector have enough gold? Did he leave an incredible legacy of glory? Did he win the girl? People treated him with kindness – perhaps that was what kept Hector moving forward through life's storms.

He was a good man, who worked hard, loved his family, his men and was compassionate to those who were struggling. My father, Henry Bagust, had a thousand stories throughout his lifetime of family memories. Yet, sadly I knew only two things passed on about my great grandfather: 'his men loved him', and, 'when there was a storm he would take his wrapped compass and bury it in the garden, afraid he could not trust himself to sail off into the ocean'.

I have worked in construction much of my life, but I have known only one or two bosses loved by their men.

As I have spent thousands of hours researching this book to tell the story as accurately as possible, I initially felt sad that these stories were all I knew. However, I have come to realise, if all you had on your gravestone was 'He was loved by his men', wouldn't that be enough?

Hector buried his compass to be with his family. At the end of the day, isn't that what really matters? That we have loved God and loved our fellow man.

I remember a friend once asking a simple question: "If you could only have one word on your gravestone, what would it be?"

Instantly my word came to mind. What is yours?

Barbara McQuarrie

Christine McLeod

Euphemia McQuarrie

Hannah McQuarrie

About the Author

Growing up in New Zealand in a rural community, I loved climbing trees or creating some peril to squeeze the last drop from my toothpaste tube of time, before dinner curtailed my wild adventures. I thought adults were boring talking by the hour about nothing. By twelve, I sat mesmerised, listening to endless passioned stories recounted in waves of loud raucous laughter. I concluded my ageing relatives were aliens from another planet as their pioneering world had little resemblance to mine. None the less, I wanted to record these stories for others to enjoy. How hard could it be, right? I'd already used words like a paintbrush writing poetry or telling bedtime stories, so why not a novel.

Travelling in 2015, I began writing about our quirky adventures, and encounters and was encouraged to write more. Adding to the thousands of hours of research my family had already done, I picked up a pen and started writing, feeling privileged to bring back to life characters from our families who left their own wonderful imprint in our DNA and on our landscape. And my brother said: "Don't let the facts get in the way of a good story."